New Beginnings
And Other Stories

ISBN: 9798645278014

CONTENTS

NEW BEGINNINGS

The schoolmaster looked sternly over the rims of his spectacles. "Settle down now and take out your copybooks and pencils," he ordered.

It was nine-thirty on a fine April morning and the start of another humdrum day of English, Irish and Arithmetic in the little village school of Dunmore. Just as order was beginning to descend on the room the door was pushed open and all heads turned to see who the latecomer was. To their delight in walked their old pal Francie McDonagh.

"Ah Francie," smiled the master, as he stood chalk in hand at the dusty old blackboard where he was writing up the first lesson of the day, "you're welcome back. Come on in and take a seat."

Every year in the middle of April the McDonagh family arrived in their brightly painted caravan and set up camp on the quiet country road outside the village. The family consisted of Dinny, his wife Winnie, and their four children Francie, Lizzie, Noreen and Sally. Like the song of the cuckoo and the primroses which decorated the roadside, their arrival was just another sign that summer was on its way.

Dinny always found plenty of work to do in the locality, mending pots, pans and buckets for the local people. When all the mending and repairing was done he'd find seasonal employment with the farmers, making hay, weeding turnips, and doing any other odd jobs that came his way. Then, when August came they'd gather up their belongings and take to the road. They wouldn't be seen again until the following April.

The children attended the local school every year for two months, from the time they arrived in April until it closed for the summer holidays at the end of June. Francie who was now twelve years old was in the senior room, while his sisters who were a few years younger where taught by the mistress in the junior room. Nobody knew where they spent the rest of the year or if they went to school at all, but that didn't seem to matter much. The schoolmaster was a great believer in education and welcomed them with open arms. In his book two months of schooling a year was better than none at all and he was always ready to give a little bit of extra help and encouragement where needed.

Francie liked going to school and learning new things. He was proud of the fact that, unlike the previous generations of his family, he could now read and write and he could answer most of the questions in the Catechism. His favourite subject of all was arithmetic. He loved working out the answers to the sums and he nearly always got them right. Secretly, he wished he could live in a house like the other children so that he could go to school all year round. He never mentioned this to his father or mother as he knew they weren't going to change their way of life; travelling was in their blood. However, he couldn't help thinking and dreaming about it.

Even though most of the farmers and other inhabitants of the area got on well with the McDonagh family there were a couple of exceptions. One of these was a farmer by the name of William Dunne. William lived with his wife, Sarah, and their four year old daughter, Bridget, on a medium size farm not far from the village. It didn't matter how busy they were or what work needed to be done, they'd never allow Dinny inside the gate. People said it wasn't William who was at fault at all but his wife; she was an out-and-out snob.

Sarah was the eldest daughter of a wealthy farmer who lived about twenty miles away. Being the eldest in the family Sarah had always thought she'd be the first to marry but it didn't work out that way. Her two younger sisters were swept off their feet before they were twenty while she sat on the shelf and waited. This did nothing for her self-esteem and she became bitter. In fact, her parents had almost given up all hope of her finding a husband. It was only with the help of a good matchmaker and a sizeable dowry they had eventually managed to get her settled at all.

Getting married did nothing to change her for the better. If anything she became even more bitter than she was before. She had only married William out of desperation. She didn't love him and she always thought she should have done better for herself. In her own mind she was always a cut above the rest, and she looked down her nose at her neighbours and even her poor unfortunate husband.

One evening about a week after they arrived in the village Francie was walking home from school alone. As he was passing by Dunne's house he spotted the little girl standing on the bank of the river which flowed down at the opposite side of the road. She was peering intently into the water. Just as the thought occurred to him that it was a dangerous place for her to be on her own, she suddenly reached out as if to catch something and fell head first into the river. Without thinking, Francie jumped in, grabbed her, and pulled her out onto the bank. Then he lifted her up in his arms and hurried as fast as he could across the road and up the yard to the door.

"Hello, hello," he called, "is there anyone at home?"

The door opened and Sarah Dunne stood there staring in shock at the scene in front of her. A few moments later she came to her senses. She recognized Francie as one of the traveller children who were staying in the caravan near the village and immediately thought the worst of him.

"What in the name of God have you done?" she demanded.

 "I haven't done anything. I was just passing by the gate when I saw her falling into the river, so I jumped in and pulled her out."

"Bring her in quick before she catches pneumonia."

Francie carried the little girl into the kitchen and left her down on a seat beside the fire. Her teeth were chattering and she was shivering all over from the cold. Her mother quickly removed her wet clothes, dried her and wrapped her up in a warm blanket. She asked Francie to go out to the haggard beside the house and tell William to come in.

"We're very grateful to you for saving our daughter" said William, "She's usually safe playing in the yard, but somebody must have left the gate open and she wandered across the road. If you hadn't come along when you did she could have drowned."

Sarah, who was busy hanging wet towels on the line above the fire, stopped what she was doing and turned on William.

"What do you mean? 'Somebody left the gate open!' I suppose it was my fault again, just like everything that goes wrong round here."

"Hold on now Sarah, nobody is blaming anyone. Let's just be thankful that Bridget is safe."

"Well, I'm glad I was able to help." said Francie as he edged towards the door, "I better go home now and get out of these wet clothes.

"Of course, of course, go on home before you catch your death."

Little Bridget was soon back to herself and was none the worse for her experience. A couple of days later William Dunne suggested to his wife that they should give young Francie McDonagh some class of a reward for saving their daughter's life. It would never have occurred to Sarah to do such a thing, but she grudgingly went along with her husband's suggestion. They decided on a sum of fifty pounds.

The Dunnes sent word to Dinny McDonagh asking him and young Francie to call up to the house. When they arrived they were brought into the kitchen. William said that he wanted to thank Francie properly for saving Bridget's life. Then he took the fifty pound note from his pocket and left it on the table near where Dinny and Francie were sitting.

"I hope you'll accept this little gift in appreciation of what your family has done for us" said William. Dinny stared at the money for a few seconds and then looked at William.

"Oh no," he said, shaking his head, "we can't take that."

"Why not?"

"Because it'd bring us nothing but bad luck."

"I don't understand. Why would it bring you bad luck?"

"Did you never hear that if you save someone's life, and you take money as a reward, you'll never have a day's luck again?"

Sarah couldn't believe what she was hearing. "Ah sure, that's only an old phisogue," she said, "surely you don't believe it".

"It's no phisogue at all," replied Dinny, "didn't I know a man who saved somebody's life and took money as a reward, three months later he was dead himself."

"So you won't take it?" asked William.

"Indeed we won't."

Dinny and Francie stood up and headed for the door.

"Hold on a minute," said William, "if you won't take the money is there anything else we can do for you."

"Well, there is," said Francie nervously, "you could give me a job."

"A job?"

"If I could stay here I could go to school all year round, not just for two months. When I'm not in school I could work on the farm, in the evenings and on Saturdays and Sundays."

Sarah was shocked when she heard this. "No," she said "that wouldn't work at all."

"Oh, I don't know "replied William, who felt that he could do with a bit of help around the farm, "maybe it's not such a bad idea. We have a spare room and there's plenty of work for Francie to do here. It's up to Dinny of course."

All eyes were now on Dinny as they waited for his reaction. He was just as shocked as Sarah. He understood that it'd be a great opportunity for Francie to get a better education, but he worried about him being separated from his family at such a young age.

"Are you sure about this Francie? he asked, "Will you not miss your family?"

"Of course, I will Dad," replied Francie, "but I really want to go to school. Anyway the months will go by quickly and I'll see you all again in the summer."

In the end, Dinny agreed to let him stay. All they had to do now was go home and break the news to his mother.

Francie continued to live with his own family for the rest of the summer, but when they moved on in August he went to live with the Dunnes. He attended school regularly and helped out on the farm in his free time. As the weeks and months went by William was happy that he had taken Francie in to live with them. He was no trouble, and it was always good to have an extra pair of hands around the place when things got busy. Sarah, on the other hand, barely tolerated him. She cooked his meals and washed his clothes, but other than that she practically ignored him. This wasn't surprising as she had very little time for anybody but herself.

Several years later Francie McDonagh was still living in the house of William Dunne. When he finished school, instead of going off and getting himself a job, he had stayed on working with William on the farm. Over the years the Dunnes had come to realise that they couldn't manage without him, so now they were paying him a good weekly wage.

As she grew up Bridget spent all her free time helping out around the farm and Francie and she spent a lot of time together. Now that she was nineteen her parents hoped she'd soon meet and marry a local farmer's son who'd take over the running of the farm after their day. However, things weren't working out as they had planned. Bridget never went dancing in the village hall or showed any interest in the local boys. Sometimes, when Sarah saw Francie and her together laughing over some private joke or other, she wondered if there was more than friendship between them. But then she'd dismiss the thought from her mind as quickly as it had come. Surely Bridget would have more sense than that.

Then one night when the three of them were sitting around the fire after supper Bridget said she had something to tell her parents. Her mother looked at her suspiciously.

"Go on, what is it?"
"I know this is going to come as a bit of a shock to you but Francie and I have been seeing each other for quite some time now, and we have decided we want to get married."

Sarah's face turned a deathly shade of pale and she looked like she was about to collapse. William rushed to get her a glass of water and she downed it in one go.

"Get married to Francie McDonagh?" she spluttered, "If you think I'm going to stand by and watch my daughter marry a traveller you must be barmy"

" No, I'm not barmy," replied Bridget, "I'm just a nineteen year old girl who wants to marry the man she loves."

"And I suppose you think the two of you are going to take over the farm. I wouldn't be surprised if you were planning on putting your father and me in the County Home."

William tried to intervene. "Hold on now Sarah, maybe we can talk this over calmly and come to some class of an agreement."

Sarah turned on her husband. "There will be no agreement. If she insists on going ahead with this harebrained idea of hers she won't be living under my roof. And just in case you're thinking of taking her side, remember this – it's either her or me. One of us will have to go. And that's my final word on the matter." She rose from her seat and stormed out of the kitchen banging the door behind her.

If there was one thing that could be said about Sarah Dunne it was that she never went back on her word. From that day on she never discussed the subject again. Bridget tried to get her father to reason with her but he said, unfortunately, there was nothing he could do. So Bridget and Francie left the farm and got a little house to rent in the village. It didn't take him too long to get another job as he had the name of being a good worker. They had a quiet wedding with only the priest and two witnesses in attendance.

After that Sarah cut them off completely as if they had never existed. William was heartbroken but what could he do? As she had said herself, it was either her or Bridget. Even when, sometime later, they became the proud parents of a baby boy, whom they called Bill after his grandfather, it still didn't do anything to soften her heart or change her mind.

As time went by it became apparent that it was Sarah herself who suffered most because of her actions. She put all her time and energy into working on the farm and gave up any interaction with the outside world. After a few years her health began to deteriorate. William tried to get her to see the doctor but she wouldn't listen to him. It was as if she was determined to work herself into an early grave. And eventually she succeeded. Five years after Bridget moved out, Sarah passed away in her sleep one night.

Bridget was shocked to hear of her mother's sudden death. She thought back to when she was very young; she had been so close to her mother then. She wondered how things could have gone so terribly wrong. Up to now there had always been the hope that one day they'd be reconciled, but sadly that would never happen now. She didn't go to the wake which was held in the house but attended the funeral along with her husband and child.

One night a couple of weeks later they decided to pay William a visit. He was delighted to see them and to meet his grandson, who was now five years old, for the first time. They all sat around the open fire drinking tea and chatting. It was almost like old times. Then William had a question to ask.

"Well, what do you say?"

"About what?" asked Bridget.

"About coming back here of course. You know if it was up to me you would never have had to leave in the first place. Unfortunately, your mother saw things differently, but I hope we can put all that behind us now and make a fresh start. It's time for me to retire anyway and let somebody else take over."

"But why did you let her have her way, Dad? Surely you could have stopped her from splitting up the family the way she did?"

"I don't know about that, Bridget. Your mother was a very stubborn woman. If you and Francie had stayed I really think she would have left.

"So you chose her over me?"

"I didn't want to choose, but when I married your mother I promised we'd be together *"till death do us part."* I just couldn't bring myself to go back on my word."

Bridget looked at Francie "What do you think?

"I think it's the best offer we're going to get and we should accept".

"Alright," said Bridget, "we accept."

William went to the cupboard and took out a bottle of whiskey and three glasses. Then he found a bottle of lemonade and poured out a glass for his grandson.

"Now, what should we drink to? he asked.

"To new beginnings," said Kate.

"To new beginnings!"

The celebrations went on for a long time and only ended when both the whiskey bottle and the lemonade bottle stood empty on the table. Then they all went home and slept soundly dreaming about new beginnings.

AN INSIDE JOB

When Kate and Thomas got married in nineteen fifty-five, they had no house of their own, so they moved in with Kate's parents for the time being. The place was a bit crowded as Kate had younger siblings still living there so they hoped to get their own place as soon as possible. Thomas was an agricultural worker who worked with the local farmers and Kate was employed as a shop assistant in the village.

One day after dinner Thomas was looking through the Farmer's Journal when, on the advertisement page, he saw some jobs on offer. As he scanned down through them, he came across one that caught his attention. '*Young couple wanted to work on a large farm in County Cork, good pay and conditions, free cottage available for suitable applicants.*' There was a name and address to write to, if interested in the positions. Thomas tore out the ad and put it in his pocket.

When he showed it to Kate that night, she agreed it was too good an opportunity to miss, so they wrote a letter and sent it off the following day. A week later they received a reply offering them a three month trial. If everything went well, they would be offered the jobs permanently when the three months was up.

The following week Thomas and Kate travelled the fifty miles to the farm and met the owner Petesy O'Reilly. Petesy was a bachelor, in his seventies, who lived alone. Both his brother and sister had passed away during the previous year, so he needed somebody to help him take care of the house and farm.

He told them about his nephew, Cormac, who lived in the village two miles away. When Cormac was a young boy, he had always helped out on the farm, and it had been Petesy's intention to leave him everything. However, things hadn't turned out as Petesy would have liked. Cormac seemed to have lost all interest in farm work. In fact, he didn't seem to like any kind of work at all. All he wanted was to get as much money as he could out of his uncle. He spent most of his time these days between the pub and the bookies. Petesy could never rely on him when he needed something done.

Thomas and Kate took up residence in the cottage and started work on the farm. Thomas worked in the fields with Petesy, while Kate did all the work in the farmhouse. About a week later, they were in the cottage after work one evening when a car pulled up outside. Thomas went to the door.

"Hello, I saw the light and wondered who was in the cottage," said the shifty-looking, young man standing on the doorstep.

"I'm Thomas O'Neill. I've just started working on the farm with Petesy. This is my wife, Kate, she's working in the farmhouse."

"So you've landed two nice cushy jobs for yourselves?"

"Who are you?"

" I'm Petesy's nephew, Cormac. I'll be taking over the farm one of these days, so I'd advise you not to get too comfortable. Do you understand?"

"We won't be taking orders from anyone except Petesy. Now if you'll excuse us, we're busy."

Thomas closed the door and Cormac got into his car and drove off up the lane towards the farmhouse. For the first time since they arrived they felt uneasy. They didn't like Cormac and thought that he could be a troublemaker. They would try to stay out of his way if they could.

As the weeks and months went by the O'Neill's settled into their new surroundings. They developed a good relationship with Petesy, and he couldn't have been happier with how things were going. It looked like this was going to be a long term arrangement. They often saw Cormac's car going up the lane to the farmhouse, but they had no further dealings with him.

Thomas and Kate were free to do whatever they wanted on Sundays. They liked to explore the area where they lived, so they often went for long walks in the afternoon. One Sunday they were almost back at the cottage, when they met Cormac driving down the lane from the farmhouse. Thomas remarked to Kate that he's probably short of money again, and he's been up to see what he can get from Petesy. When they went in to the cottage, it was six o'clock. Thomas turned on the wireless to get the news and Kate set about preparing the supper. They were looking forward to a nice quiet evening to themselves.

The following morning they were both up early as usual. After breakfast they tidied up the kitchen, and set out for the farmhouse to begin their day's work. When they arrived in Petesy's yard, there was no sign of anyone around. This was unusual. Petesy was an early bird; he was always out and about when they got there. He'd be feeding the hens or tiding up around the place. He was never a man to sleep on in the morning.

Feeling a bit uneasy they went to the door and found it wasn't locked. Thomas lifted the latch and pushed in the door. He walked into the kitchen, with Kate following close behind him. They couldn't believe their eyes at the scene that greeted them. There, sitting on a chair in the middle of the room was Petesy. His arms and legs were tied to the chair and, a piece of cloth had been stuffed into his mouth. His head hung to one side and his eyes were closed. At first they didn't know if he was asleep, unconscious or worse.

When Thomas went over to him and called his name, he slowly opened his eyes and stared at him. Thomas told him not to worry; he was going to be alright now. He gently removed the cloth from Petesy's mouth and then got a knife and cut the ropes that bound him to the chair. Both of them helped the old man over to the armchair beside the fire. Kate made him a cup of strong tea with plenty of sugar. She told him to sip it slowly; it'd help to revive him. When he had drunk the tea, Petesy looked better, but he was very confused about what had happened the previous evening

All he could remember was a masked man, with a stout stick in his hand, standing in front of him, demanding money. After being hit a couple of times about the arms and shoulders, he had told the intruder there was some money upstairs in a drawer. The assailant then proceeded to tie Petesy to the chair and went up the stairs. Petesy said he could hear him pulling out drawers and throwing them on the ground. Then he came back down the stairs and went out the door leaving Petesy tied to the chair.   It had been a long night for poor Petesy. He had dozed off a few times, but most of the night he had been awake. The only thing that kept him going was the knowledge that Thomas and Kate would arrive early in the morning; all he had to do was hold on until then.

Thomas cycled to the village to report the incident to the guards while Kate stayed to look after Petesy.

He also went to Cormac's house and told him what had happened to his uncle. An hour later Thomas returned in the squad car with the Sergeant and a young guard from the village. Petesy told the guards the same story he had told Thomas and Kate earlier. Then they asked Thomas and Kate what they knew about the incident. Thomas told them they had met Cormac driving away from the farmhouse, when they were returning from their walk the previous evening. They knew no more until they came up this morning and found the old man tied to the chair in the kitchen.

"Have you any idea what time you saw Cormac driving away from the farmhouse?" asked the Sergeant.

"It was about five to six. I know that because when I went in to the kitchen and turned on the wireless, the six o'clock news was just starting."

Just then they heard a car pulling up outside. Cormac rushed into the kitchen full of concern for his uncle. The Sergeant asked him what he knew about the events of the previous evening.

"Well," said Cormac, "I called up here to see my uncle at five o'clock yesterday evening. I spent about an hour talking to him in the kitchen, and when I left, he was in his usual good form. The intruder must have come later in the evening."

The old man was still confused. He couldn't remember Cormac visiting him at all. The only thing he could remember was a masked man standing in front of him, demanding money. Nor had he any idea at what time the robbery had taken place. Just as the guards were about to leave, the Sergeant turned to Petesy and asked him if there was anything else at all he could remember. Petesy thought for a moment.

"Well there is something, it mightn't be important, but it's about my watch."

"What about your watch?"

"I was wearing an old watch, which had belonged to my father. When the intruder hit me with the stick, I heard the glass crack and the watch flew off my arm. It wasn't hard to knock it off; the strap was worn to a thread. I had meant to replace it but had never got around to it.

"And where is it now?

"I don't know, it must be on the floor somewhere," said Petesy, looking around "I didn't get a chance to look for it yet".

They searched the kitchen for the watch but there was no sign of it anywhere. As a last resort, the young guard took a torch out of his pocket, got down on the floor and peered in under the dresser. Sure enough, there, amidst the dust and cobwebs, was the watch that Petesy was talking about. He pulled it out and handed it to the Sergeant.

"Oh, you found it," said Petesy, "is it still working?"

"No, I'm afraid it's not working Petesy," said the Sergeant. "But that's not important at the moment. What's important is the time that it stopped at."

"Well, don't keep us in suspense", said Petesy. "What time did it stop?"

"It stopped at twenty minutes to six."

You could hear a pin drop in the kitchen. All eyes turned to Cormac who was trying to edge his way towards the door. The Sergeant informed him they were arresting him for the assault and robbery of his uncle and took him away in the squad car.

Petesy was shocked when he realised he had been assaulted and robbed by his own nephew. He had known for a long time that Cormac was up to no good, but he never thought he would stoop this low. He would never let him anywhere near the farm again. He asked Thomas and Kate if they would move into the farmhouse with him, as he was nervous about staying on his own after what had happened. A month later Petesy told them that he would like them to accompany him to see his solicitor.

"Why are you going to see the solicitor?" asked Thomas.

"Because I want to make over the house and farm to you and Kate."

They were both stunned by this announcement. "Are you sure Petesy?" asked Thomas, "We don't want you to feel under any pressure to leave the place to us."

"Well, I'm certainly not leaving it to that good-for-nothing nephew of mine, and there are no two people I'd rather leave it to than Kate and yourself. And sure who knows, maybe you'll have a son or daughter to pass it on to after your day."

"Actually, there's something we've been meaning to tell you," said Kate. "But so much has been happening lately, we didn't get a chance. In a few months from now, we'll be having an addition to the family."

Petesy's eyes lit up with delight. "That's the best news I've heard in a long time", he smiled, "All the more reason for us to go to the solicitor and get things sorted out. The day I got that letter from you two, I had a feeling that everything was going to work out, and it's beginning to look like I was right."

THE LONG FISHING TRIP

As Emily O'Connor danced the night away in the National ballroom in Dublin in the summer of nineteen-fifty, she had a feeling that her life was about to change forever. Earlier in the night she had been sitting with her friends, when she noticed a tall good-looking young man coming towards them. Emily was sure he'd ask one of the others to dance but was delighted when he chose her. He said his name was Peter Doherty and he worked as a primary school teacher in the city. That was the beginning of their romance.

Emily, who was twenty-five years old, worked in a large Department Store in the city centre. She loved her work and enjoyed socialising with her friends. However, she had never had a serious boyfriend before. They had only been going out a short time when she knew that Peter was the love of her life and he felt the same about her. They both knew that it was only a matter of time before they'd get married.

Even though they had been born and reared in the city, they both had a great love of the outdoors. Any free time they had was spent walking in the Dublin or Wicklow mountains. Emily also loved drawing and painting, and she often brought her paints and brushes with her on their trips to the countryside. It was no surprise to anyone when, about eight months after they had first met, they got engaged. Both families were happy for them and Emily proudly showed off her ring to her colleagues at work.

"What are we going to do to celebrate our engagement?" asked Peter.

"I don't know," replied Emily, "maybe we could go down to Wicklow or Wexford for a week-end."

"I have a better idea, why don't we take a trip to the West of Ireland. It'd be something different. Walking, swimming, fishing, just imagine all the things we could do, and it'd be a great chance for you to catch up on some painting as well."

This seemed like a great idea. The Easter break would be coming up soon and they both had some time off from work, so they decided to go away for a whole week. It took some time to find accommodation but eventually they got it sorted. They were going to a small seaside resort off the coast of Mayo. The brochure in the travel agents said it was a charming little village surrounded by mountains, cliffs and sea; it sounded idyllic and they couldn't wait to get there.

As the train sped through the midlands bringing them to the west, they talked about all the things they were going to do during the week; they were both looking forward to a whole week away from the hustle and bustle of city life. When they finally arrived at their destination they weren't disappointed. The scenery was breathtaking; neither of them had ever seen anything like it before. The rugged mountains and cliffs and the wild Atlantic Ocean beating off the rocks took their breath away.

It didn't take Emily and Peter long to settle in to their new surroundings. They spent the first couple of days exploring the numerous walking trails in the area. In the evening they'd have a meal in a local restaurant and chat about what they had seen on their stroll that day. One evening, as they were walking back to their accommodation, they came to a little pier where several fishing boats were moored for the night.

"Look," said Peter, "there's a sign that says boats for hire." Why don't we take one out tomorrow and try our hand at fishing?"

It was true that Emily liked most outdoor pursuits, but a boat-trip wasn't one of them. Years earlier, when she was at a seaside resort with her family, they had taken a trip in a boat. She had somehow managed to fall into the sea and almost drowned. That was the last time she had been in a boat and she didn't relish the idea of going out in one now.

"I have a better idea," she said. You take the boat

out on your own. I'll take my paints and brushes up to the top of the cliff and paint a picture of the boat sailing out from the pier. We'll always keep it as a reminder of our trip to Mayo."

The following morning they were both up early. Emily headed up the cliff with her painting equipment while Peter made his way down to the pier. Half an hour later she was making a rough sketch of the boat as it moved slowly out from the pier. When it eventually disappeared from sight she was happy that she had got the outline she required. Now, she could spend the rest of the day filling in the surrounding details and completing the painting.

A couple of hours later Emily was still on the cliff top when there was a sudden change in the weather. It had been a lovely sunny morning, but now the sky darkened and it was already starting to rain. She gathered up her paints and brushes and quickly made her way down to the village. She had just got back to the hotel when there was a flash of lightening followed immediately by a clap of thunder. That was when she started to worry; she hoped Peter hadn't gone out too far in the boat and that he'd be able to get back in safely. As soon as the rain eased off she'd go down to the pier to see if there was any sign of him.

That was the start of the longest evening of Emily's life. The thunder and lightning continued for hours along with torrential rain and wind. She was really scared now. The lady at reception tried to reassure her, saying that Peter was probably waiting down at the pier for the storm to abate before coming back to the hotel. Emily prayed that she was right. However, as the hours dragged by there was no sign of him. About eight o'clock the rain eased off enough for Emily to make her way down to the pier. When she asked the man who rented the boats if Peter had returned from his fishing trip, he told her that there was no sign of him. All the boats which were out that day had come back except Peter's. Emily was distraught; it looked like her worst fears were about to come true.

Early the following morning lifeboats were dispatched to look for the missing boat. They travelled for miles up and down the coastline and searched all islands in the area but, unfortunately, nothing was found. After a week the search was called off and Emily was told there was nothing more they could do. Peter was presumed to have perished in one of the worst storms to hit the area in many years.

Emily was devastated. All she could do was gather up their belongings and return to Dublin. However, she refused to believe that Peter was dead. She hoped he had somehow managed to survive the storm and one day they would find each other again. Then everything could go back to how it was before; they'd get married and live a happy life together. She would never give up hope. Every year on the anniversary of the tragedy, Emily went down to the little seaside village in Mayo and had a Mass said for Peter. She'd climb up to the cliff-top, gaze out over the bay, and let her mind wander back to that sunny morning when she had, unknowingly at the time, watched that tiny fishing-boat taking her loved one away from her, perhaps forever.

As the years passed Emily concentrated on her career and was eventually promoted to manager of her department. She occasionally socialised with her friends but never had another boyfriend. How could she? For all she knew, Peter might still be alive. As long as that possibility was there, she'd never get involved with anyone again. When her siblings married and had children she became very close to her nieces and nephews. She would often baby-sit and help take care of them. In time, she became everyone's favourite auntie.

When Emily retired she went to live with one of her nieces, Jennifer, who was married and had two children. At first she worried she might be in the way, but she soon became part of the family. She got on great with the children and they loved spending time with her. Unfortunately, she didn't have much time with them. Three years after her retirement, at the age of sixty-eight, after a short illness she passed away.

Shortly after this, Jennifer's youngest son started college so she found herself with lots of spare time on her hands. She had always wanted to do voluntary work so she made enquiries. She came across an organisation that was looking for people to visit hospital patients who had no relatives or friends of their own. She thought this sounded like a worthwhile endeavour so she decided to give it a try.

Over the next couple of months Jennifer visited several patients. She loved chatting to them and hearing their stories; there was so much to be learned from them. One day the matron asked her if she'd drop in on an elderly patient called Christopher who didn't have any visitors since he came to the hospital two weeks ago. After chatting for a while Jennifer asked him where he was from.

"I'm from Kerry," he said", "well at least that's where I've lived for over forty years."

"And what about your family, do you have relatives in Kerry?"

The old man smiled "You might find it hard to believe, but I haven't a relative in the world."

"But that's impossible!" exclaimed Jennifer. "Sure everyone has relatives of some sort; whether they get on with them or not is another thing."

"Well, I suppose you're right in a way, but when you hear my story you'll understand what I mean.

Christopher told her that the first memory he had was of waking up in a hospital bed in Tralee surrounded by doctors and nurses. They told him he had been found unconscious in a small fishing boat which had washed up on the shore. He was brought to the hospital where he had remained unconscious for three months. Once he regained consciousness several tests were carried out and it was confirmed that his memory had been completely erased. The rest of his brain seemed to be working fine and the doctors reassured him that in time his memory would probably come back. Unfortunately, they were wrong; his memory never returned. It was as if his life had begun on that day in nineteen fifty-one, even though he must have been in his late twenties at the time.

"The hospital authorities tried their best to find out who I was, but without success. I eventually went to live with a family near Tralee where I worked on the farm all my life. A month ago I had a heart attack and was sent up here to have an operation. Now you know what I mean when I say I haven't a relative in the world."

"So how did you come to be called Christopher?"

"Well, the only thing I had in my possession when I was found, apart from my clothes, was a silver medal on a chain around my neck. The nurses told me it was a medal of St Christopher and that he had saved me from the sea. It was their suggestion that I should adopt the name Christopher and I went along with it."

Jennifer thought this was the saddest story she had ever heard in her life. She felt like crying but then the old man smiled at her.

"Don't look so sad," he said, "all that happened a long time ago and, considering everything, I've had a reasonably good life. Now that I've told you all about the family I don't have, maybe you can tell me something about the family you do have."

Jennifer told him all about her family; then she had an idea. "Would you like me to bring in some photos of my family next time?"
"That would be great; I'll look forward to seeing them."

The following week, before going to visit Christopher, Jennifer gathered up some photos of her family and put them in her bag. As soon as she arrived he asked if she had brought them. She was surprised as she thought the old man would have forgotten all about them. As she passed the photos to him one by one, she explained who was in them. There were pictures of her parents, brothers and sisters and her own husband and children. Lastly, she came to one of her Aunt Emily, which was taken when she was a young girl in her twenties. "This is my Aunt Emily, who passed away last year" said Jennifer as she handed the photo to Christopher. When she gave him the other photos he had commented on each one; however, this time there was silence. When Jennifer looked at him she was amazed to see he was staring intently at the photo with tears in his eyes.

"What's wrong Christopher?" she asked
"There's nothing wrong. It's just the girl in this photo ... she looks so... so beautiful! The reason I never married was that I felt I never met the right girl. But I can tell you that if I had met this young lady forty years ago, I wouldn't have let her out of my

sight for a moment."

Jennifer was amused by his reaction to the photo. She thought it so romantic that the old man should fall in love with a picture of her beloved Aunt Emily. As she gathered up the photos to put them in her bag Christopher asked her if he could keep that one, and she agreed as she had several other photos of her aunt at home.

From then on, Christopher kept the photo on his little bedside table, and every night he slept with it under his pillow. Unfortunately, his condition deteriorated and one night a few weeks later he passed away in his sleep. When the nurse came on her rounds she found him with the photo clutched tightly to his chest and a peaceful smile on his face.

THE MATCHMAKER

Danny Sheehan was a widower who lived in the village of Knockadoon in a remote part of the West of Ireland. His wife, Peggy, had passed away two years earlier, and he had taken her death badly as they'd been happily married for forty years. Only in the past couple of months was he beginning to be seen out and about again. Now that he was retired and living alone he found that he had a lot of time on his hands, so he began to wonder if there was something he could do to pass the time and maybe make a few pounds to supplement his pension at the same time.

One day as he was walking up the street he spotted two elderly bachelor farmers from the locality chatting on the corner. They had both come in on their bicycles from the surrounding townlands for their weekly provisions. As he passed by them he thought, how neglected and uncared for they looked; what a lonely life they must be living in their little houses out there in the countryside.

Later as he was having his tea he thought again about the two men he had seen earlier. They're not the only ones either, he thought; there must be at least twenty bachelors living in a three mile radius of the village, all in need of a good woman to look after them. Wouldn't it be great if I could set up a little match-making business, he thought. Not only would I be doing a service to the community, but I might make a few pounds for myself as well.

Danny decided the best thing to do was go down and have a word with Fr. Maguire about his idea. He was, after all, the spiritual caretaker of everyone in the parish, and it wouldn't do to go behind his back, especially where matters of courtship and marriage were concerned.

"Hello Danny, how can I help you?" asked Fr. Maguire.

"Well, I have an idea I'd like to run past you Father, if you don't mind.

"Of course not, come on in."

Danny explained the reason for his visit.

"That's not a bad idea at all now. Sure the population of the parish is going down all the time. In fact, if we don't have more children enrolling in the school soon we'll be in danger of losing a teacher. How do you propose to go about this matchmaking business? As far as I can see you have plenty of potential male clients in the parish, but what are you going to do for women?"

"Well, I was thinking maybe I could bring them in from America, Father. There must be plenty of single women over there that'd jump at the chance of marriage to an Irish bachelor. What do you think?"

"It might work. Sure there's no harm in giving it a try anyway."

Danny made out an advertisement looking for single women interested in matrimony and posted it off to an Irish/American magazine. Next he had to start getting some of the local bachelors on his books. The first he approached was Little Crooked Paddy who lived down a long boreen, had a snug house and a tidy bit of land. Paddy was a placid sort who got along well with his neighbours. His only drawback was that he had a hump on his back. For that reason he had never bothered with women and they had never bothered with him.

"I'm setting up a little matchmaking business Paddy" said Danny, "would you be interested in putting your name on the books?"

"Oh I don't know," replied Paddy, "I think I'm getting a bit long in the tooth for that kind of thing now."

"Not at all, you're never too old for love."

"How much would it cost me?" asked Paddy, scratching his head.

"Just five pounds to sign up and if you find a wife, fifty pounds to be paid on the day of the wedding".

"I suppose that's not too bad, put me down." said Paddy, as if he was buying a ticket for a raffle. Then he went down to the dresser and searched behind the willow-patterned plates until he found a fiver.

Next on the list was Long Ned of the Hill. Ned was a good-looking man, tall and thin, as his name implied, with slightly greying hair. He would have been any woman's fancy. However, Ned too had a drawback; he was the most contrary man that ever lived. If you said something was black, he'd say it was white; if you said it was good, he'd say it was bad, and so on. He had never yet been known to agree with anyone about anything which was most likely the reason he had never married. However, he too signed up with Danny and paid his fiver.

The third bachelor Danny visited was Black Peter who lived near the cross-roads. Peter was a backward sort of fellow. His mother died when he was young and he had been reared by his father. He was alright in the company of men, but he wasn't used to women at all. He had no idea how to behave in their presence; in fact, he almost regarded them as a different species altogether. It was little surprise, therefore, that he had never married.

When Danny brought up the subject of matchmaking he refused point blank to have anything to do with it. But when it was patiently pointed out to him that this might be his one and only chance of finding love he agreed to put down his name. Danny was pleased with the way things were going. He now had his first three gentlemen clients on his books, and he had an ad in an Irish/American magazine seeking suitable ladies.

Two weeks later the first letter arrived from America. It was from a lady in her early forties called Susan. She said her great-grandparents came from Ireland but didn't know which part. She was looking for a nice respectable Irish man to settle down with and hoped Danny would be able to help her. There would be no problem paying the hundred pounds fee when the wedding was over and the register signed. There was a photo enclosed. Susan was a good-looking woman. Maybe too good-looking, thought Danny, for the trio I have on my books!

After careful consideration, Danny wrote back enclosing a head and shoulders photo of Little Crooked Paddy. He explained that, in his opinion, this was the most suitable candidate he had on his books. If she was interested, the next step would be for her to take a trip to Ireland to meet the said gentleman in person.

Two weeks later Susan arrived in Ireland. Danny met her at the train station and brought her to the hotel. He arranged to call for her the following day to drive her out to see Paddy. When they got to the house the door was open as it was a beautiful summer's day. Danny knocked on the open door and sauntered into the kitchen followed by Susan. He introduced them and Paddy invited Susan to sit down.

After a few minutes William announced he was taking a stroll down the road to stretch his legs; he'd leave the two of them to have a bit of a chat and get to know each other better.

Half an hour later he returned. As soon as Susan heard him coming she jumped to her feet and announced she was ready to leave. Danny was a bit taken aback. Things mustn't have gone too well. As they drove back to the hotel he asked her how they had got on.

"Not very well," said Susan crossly. "You never told me that Paddy had a hump on his back."

"No, I didn't think it was important."

"Well, it is. I don't mean any disrespect to the poor man, but I didn't come all this way to marry a hunchback. Now, do you have anyone else on your books that might suit me?"

"Of course I do," replied Danny, "we're not beaten yet."

The next candidate for the position was Long Ned. Again Danny called to the hotel for Susan and drove her out to Ned's house. She was very impressed by his appearance. Here, she thought, is someone I could possibly spend the rest of my life with. Once he had introduced them Danny said he had a few calls to make and he'd come back for her in an hour.

Things went smoothly enough at first, but it wasn't long until she began to see the contrary side of Ned's nature. He contradicted everything she said. She said it was warm, he said it was cold. She said the wallpaper was blue, he said it was green. She admired the view from the window, but he said it was nothing spectacular. Eventually she gave up. She could never spend her life with this man. Life was too short to be constantly arguing with someone.

When she informed him that she wasn't interested in Ned, Danny told her not to worry. He had another client on his books that would surely suit her. The following day he brought her out to the house of Black Peter. Everything was fine as long as Danny was there. Peter was very polite. It was only when he left them alone that the trouble started. Poor Peter had never been alone in the house with a woman before and he was very nervous. Danny was only gone out the door when, without a word of warning, he grabbed her in a big bear hug and tried to kiss her. Susan managed to escape from his grasp and ran out the door calling for Danny to rescue her.

"What's wrong?" asked Danny when he heard the commotion.

"Get me out of here as quick as you can" she replied. "I'm not having anything to do with that maniac. As soon as you turned your back he was all over me like a rash. It's lucky you weren't gone too far; God only knows what would have happened."

Danny drove her back to the hotel. "Well Susan, I'm afraid we've run out of options. I'm sorry things didn't work out in your favour. I suppose the only thing you can do now is go back to America."

"Actually," she replied, smiling shyly at him, "There might be one more option."

"Oh, what's that?"

"Maybe I could marry you!"

"Begob, I never thought of that, but I suppose you could."

"What do you say?"

"Well, after coming all this way to find a husband I'd hate to see you going back disappointed, so I suppose I better say yes."

A few days later Danny met Father Maguire on the street.

"How is the match-making going Danny?" he asked.

"It's not going well at all Father. In fact, I'm giving it up. I couldn't get any of those auld bachelors fixed up at all. The only good thing to come out of it all is that I'm getting married myself."

"I'm delighted to hear it. Maybe we'll soon have a couple of new pupils to enrol in the school after all."

"You'd never know Father," smiled Danny, "I suppose it's not beyond the bounds of possibility."

ACROSS THE YEARS

It was coming up to Christmas and Eileen Burke had a lot on her mind. She was eighteen years old and had finished school the previous summer. Her mother had been a bank clerk before she married, and she persuaded Eileen to take up the same career. She had already passed the entrance exam and interview and was due to begin work in the bank in the nearby town on the 1st of February. Her parents were delighted. Eileen was an only child and they were glad she wouldn't have to leave home when she started work. However, Eileen, herself, wasn't so sure. From the time she was a small child she had always wanted to be a nurse. Her mother, however, didn't want to hear about it. She was convinced that her daughter should follow in her footsteps.

Eileen was up early on the day before Christmas Eve. Her mother always kept her busy in the house on that day and this year wouldn't be any different. There'd be cleaning, baking and cooking to be done. She hoped that by making an early start she'd have some free time in the afternoon when she could get out for a walk to clear her head.

Around two o'clock in the afternoon when all her work was done Eileen told her mother she was going out. She put on her jacket and walking shoes and headed off up the narrow mountain road. As she walked briskly along she began to think about her predicament. She wished she had somebody she could ask for advice. Eileen was so deep in thought that she didn't notice the time passing. As she suddenly became aware of her surroundings, she realised she had gone further than usual from home. I must have been walking for a couple of hours, she thought, even though she had no watch to check the time. At this stage the road had shrunk to a rugged path which went right up the side of the mountain. There were no ditches now, just rocks strewn here and there in all directions.

As she stood there, thinking she should probably turn around now and head for home, she gazed about her. At first she could see no sign of life except a couple of sheep grazing away in the distance. Then something else caught her eye. About two hundred yards away from her, she was amazed to see an old woman shuffling along with a bundle of sticks on her back. As she stood there watching her, the old woman suddenly tripped and fell. Eileen was appalled. She couldn't just leave her there; she'd have to help her.

Eileen left the path and made her way as quickly as she could through the rocks and heather until she reached the old woman who was still lying on the ground. With Eileen's help she managed to get up and sit on a rock. She looked pale and shaken, but luckily, didn't seem to have any broken bones. Eileen introduced herself, and the woman said her name was Nan.

"Where do you live?" asked Eileen

Nan pointed up the side of the mountain. "Up there," she said.

Eileen could just make out the outline of a tiny house away in the distance. "Do you think you'll be able to walk there if I help you?"

"I'm sure I will. It's very good of you to help me. I don't know what I would have done if you hadn't come along just now."

When she had rested for a few minutes Nan got to her feet. Eileen took her arm and the two of them slowly made their way in the direction of the house. After stopping a few times along the way to catch their breath, they finally got there. They went inside and Eileen helped Nan into an old armchair beside the fire. Then she set about making her something to eat. By the time she had finished she realised with a shock it had grown dark outside and she'd never be able to find her way home. Her parents would be worried sick but there was nothing she could do now.

She reckoned it'd be safer to stay here for the night and go home first thing in the morning.

After they had their tea Nan and Eileen sat beside the fire. She found the old woman easy to talk to and before she realised it she was telling her all about her problem. Nan listened patiently to what she had to say.

"I know you don't want to disappoint your parents," said Nan, "and I'm sure they only want what they think is best for you. However, life isn't always as simple as that. If you're convinced that nursing is the right career for you, then that's what you must do. And by the way, I know we have only just met, but judging by the way you've taken care of me today, I think you would make a wonderful nurse."

Eileen was relieved to hear what the old woman had to say. In fact, she felt as if a weight had been lifted from her shoulders. The following morning she was up early making breakfast for the two of them. She told Nan she'd have to go home straight away before her parents had the whole village out looking for her.

"How are you feeling today?" she asked Nan.
"I'm much better now, thanks to you."
"Will you be alright here on your own?"
"Of course I will. I've been here on my own a long time now. You go on home and have a lovely Christmas with your father and mother. They must be out of their minds with worry."

Before she left she promised Nan she'd come back to see her as soon as possible. Then she headed for home. Even in the broad daylight she had difficulty finding her way. First she had to get back to the spot where she had first seen Nan. After taking several wrong turns and going round in circles a few times, she eventually found the path and started the long descent back down the mountain. She arrived home just as her father was leaving the house to report her disappearance to the Gardaí.

"Where in the name of God have you been?" he asked. "Your mother and I have been nearly out of our minds with worry."

Eileen explained to her father what had happened. She was sorry for causing distress but there was no way she could have returned home the previous night. When things calmed down a bit her father asked her where exactly this old lady's house was. He said he had been all over the mountain several times in the past but he had never seen a house up there. She tried to explain the location of the house as best she could, but her father was still puzzled as to its whereabouts.

It was now Christmas Eve and Eileen couldn't stop thinking about Nan. She wondered how the old lady could spend Christmas on her own way up there in that isolated place. Then she had an idea.

"Dad," she asked, "will you come up with me tomorrow to Nan's house? I can't bear the thought of her being there over Christmas all on her own."

Her father agreed. Wasn't it as good a way as any to spend Christmas day? About 10 o'clock in the morning the two of them set off walking up the mountain road. It was a cold sunny morning and they hadn't gone far when Eileen decided to put on her gloves. However, when she reached into her pocket, she discovered that one of them was missing; she must have lost it the previous day.

Eileen and her father continued walking up the mountain. When they got near the top they looked around but could see no sign of the house anywhere. Soon they came to a large pile of rocks where she spotted the missing glove. When they looked closer they realised that it was the ruins of an old house which must have been deserted many years before.

"This is very strange," said Eileen's father, "but as far as I can see this is the nearest thing to a house there is up here."

Eileen said nothing; she was totally confused. Where was Nan's house; the house she had spent the night in? A short while later they turned around and made their way back down the mountain. Eileen's father suggested they should go to the village and have a word with old Tom Murphy. Tom was over ninety years old. He had lived in the village all his life and was renowned for his sharp memory. If anyone knew who lived up on the mountain now, or in the past, it'd be him. The following day the two of them went down to the village to see Tom.

"Is there anyone living up near the top of the

mountain?" asked Eileen's father.

"Indeed there's not. Sure nobody would live in a place like that now, it's too remote."

"Who was the last to live up there?"

"Let me see now," said Tom "As yes, Donnellys I think they were called. There was a big family there at one time. I remember them going to school. All of them, except one of the girls, emigrated to America. Sure they had to go in those days; there was nothing for them here."

"Do you know anything about the one who didn't emigrate? What became of her?"

"She was the youngest so she stayed there to look after the father and mother in their old age. That was the way in those days. After the old people died she lived on her own for a few years. Just before Christmas one year she was out gathering sticks for the fire when she slipped and fell among the rocks. A couple of young lads out walking on Christmas Day found her body. It was very sad; she died all alone with no one to help her."

"Do you by any chance remember her name?"

"I do indeed, it was Nan."

They didn't need to hear anymore so they thanked Tom for the information and left. Eileen and her parents sat up late into the night talking about her experience but could make no sense of it whatsoever. In the end they came to a decision. They would never mention it again, either among themselves or to anyone else. The best thing they reckoned was to forget that it ever happened.

Two weeks later Eileen told her parents she had made a decision; she wasn't going to take up the job in the bank. Her parents were horrified.

"You can't be serious!" said her mother, "you might never get an opportunity like this again."
"I'm sorry mother," replied Eileen, "but I don't want to work in a bank; I'm going to become a nurse."

It took a lot of persuasion on Eileen's part, but eventually they gave her their blessing, and she went off to Dublin to begin her training. She remained in the nursing profession for over forty years and never once regretted her decision. Over the years she often thought about old Nan. She never came any closer to understanding what happened that night. All she knew was that somehow an old woman had reached across the years to help a young girl make the most important decision of her life and for that Eileen would always be grateful.

THE POITÍN MAKERS

A hundred years ago Ireland was a very different place from what it is today. People were poor and life was hard. In this respect the parish of Kilmore in County Galway was no different from anywhere else. Kilmore was a medium-sized parish consisting of a village and a cluster of townlands. The population was made up mainly of small farmers and labourers who lived in cottages.

In those days people worked hard from morning till night just to feed and clothe themselves and their children. Luxuries were unheard of. The people of Kilmore, however, had one advantage over many other parishes in the district; they had a plentiful supply of poitín. Despite recent efforts by both Church and State to rid the country of this terrible scourge, there were still at least ten poitín stills in operation throughout the parish. No matter how bad times got the people of Kilmore could always be sure of "a drop of the craythur" to ease their aches and pains and lift their weary spirits.

The poitín makers of Kilmore were lucky. The two guards who were stationed in the village were partial to a drop of the stuff themselves and therefore turned a blind eye to the making of it. Any time the excise men came sniffing around the guards would manage to head them off in a different direction. Apart from the guards, the other person who could have caused trouble for them was the parish priest, Fr. McLoughlin. Here again they were lucky. Fr. McLoughlin was a saintly man in his eighties who was dearly beloved by his parishioners. He was a bit senile, however, and wasn't aware of half the things that were going on in the parish, so the poitín makers had no trouble from him either.

Sooner or later, however, all good things come to an end. One Sunday as Fr. McLoughlin was saying Mass he had a heart attack and died. His parishioners were heartbroken. They knew they'd never be lucky enough to get anyone like him again. Soon after the funeral rumours started going round about the new priest coming to Kilmore. They said he was a man of about forty who was very authoritative in his manner. The bishop was sending him to Kilmore to "clean up" the parish. Old Fr. McLoughlin had been in charge for too long, with the result that matters of faith and morals had become very lax; now was the time for a complete overhaul.

The following week the new priest, Fr. O'Leary, arrived in the village. The first few Sundays everything went smoothly enough. He said he was happy to be in Kilmore and he looked forward to getting acquainted with the people. They began to relax and thought maybe he's not too bad after all. Then on the fourth Sunday everything changed. From the moment he ascended the pulpit and peered at them over the tops of his spectacles, they all knew he had something serious on his mind.

"There are going to be a few changes in this parish," he announced, "now that I am in charge. The first problem I am going to deal with is the poitín. From this day on both its making and consumption within the parish is completely banned. It's now the beginning of October. This year, with the help of God, you're all going to have a sober Christmas. Instead of spending your money on the Devil's drink as you've done in the past, this year you're going to spend it on your children. On Christmas morning I want to see every child in this parish properly dressed in a warm coat and a good pair of shoes, and if I get as much as a whiff of poitín from anyone, man or woman, the consequences will be very severe indeed."

The people of the parish were dumbfounded. They had expected that the new priest wouldn't be in favour of excessive consumption of poitín, but banning it outright – this was unbelievable. Poitín had been part of their lives for hundreds of years, passed down from generation to generation. They couldn't see how it could be wiped out overnight; it just wouldn't work.

In the weeks following Fr. O'Leary's sermon there was much secretive discussion on the subject throughout the parish. Eventually a plan was put in place. A meeting would be held at a secret location to decide what to do. All interested parties were invited to attend. Word quickly spread around the parish. On the night of the meeting about thirty people turned up. The discussion went on for a long time but they didn't appear to be getting any nearer to a solution.

Just as they were about to abandon the meeting, a young lad, called Owen, who was as fond as the next man of a drop of poitín, raised his hand and said he had an idea that might work.

"You all remember how Fr. O'Leary referred to poitín as "the Devil's drink," well maybe we can use that to our advantage."

Owen explained his plan. He would dress up as the devil with a red suit and horns on his head. He'd get about ten other young fellows to act as his helpers or fellow devils. At the centre of the parish was a hillock which could be seen from all directions. They'd go up at midnight, light a huge fire and, dressed in their devil outfits and with the help of a good supply of poitín, they'd party through the night.

Meanwhile, down in the village, the people would draw Fr. O'Leary's attention to the fire, advising him to go up to see what was happening. When he went up and saw the devil and his cohorts dancing around the fire, he'd get such a fright that they'd have no bother making a bargain with him. Everyone agreed that this was a great idea and Owen was pronounced a genius on the spot.

The next couple of weeks were a busy time for Owen and his friends. Among other things, outfits had to be assembled and fuel for the fire had to be collected and brought to the chosen spot. When everything was ready they decided on a night and informed their associates in the village.

As midnight approached the whole village had its eyes fixed on the little hillock. At first the fire appeared like a tiny pinhead of light in the distance. But as they watched it quickly grew bigger and bigger until the whole sky seemed to be alight. A couple of men ran to Fr. O'Leary's house to alert him.

"What do you think it means?" he asked.
"I don't know Father," answered one of them, but if you want my advice, I think it'd be better for you to go up there yourself and investigate, it could be something serious."

Fr. O'Leary instructed one of the men to saddle up his horse. Then he set off out the road in the direction of the fire, with a large crowd of people following on foot. When they got to the top of the hill there was a ditch which blocked their view. The priest dismounted from his horse and, along with a few of the men, climbed up the side of the ditch and peered over the top.   There in full view was the devil surrounded by a group of lesser demons. The devil himself was dressed in red with a large pair of horns sticking out of his head. The others were dressed from head to toe in black. In one hand they held pitchforks with which they fed and poked the fire. In the other hand they each had a bottle of poitín. There was much singing, laughing and screeching.

As the priest stood there, taking in the scene before him, the group around the fire suddenly spotted him. They stopped what they were doing and stood staring in his direction. Then the devil spoke.

"Oh, so you've come to join us Father, that's very kind of you." He laughed demonically and all the others joined in.

"In the name of God what do you want?" asked the priest, trying to sound braver than he felt."

"We'd just like to make a little bargain with you, if you don't mind."

"Go on, I'm listening."

"Well, it's like this. The good people of this parish have been partaking of my drink for many years now, and no one has come to any harm because of it. I know you're thinking of the children and how the money could be better spent on them rather than on the drink. But I don't think it's a good idea for you to come in and ban it outright. In fact, I can't allow it."

"Well, what do you want me to do then?"

"Maybe we can come to an agreement. Both production and consumption of poitín in the parish will be reduced by half. That way there'll be more money to spend on the children, and the men and women will still be able to enjoy a little tipple now again. What do you say?"

"I agree, providing you stay away from this parish from now on and let me get on with my job."

"It's a deal."

Without another word Fr. O'Leary slid down the side of the ditch, mounted his horse and headed for home. He was livid, but what could he do? The devil was no man to argue with. I'll go along with him for now, he thought, but he needn't think the fight is over. After Christmas I'll redouble my efforts, so that by this time next year there won't be a drop of poitín to be found anywhere in the parish.

The following Sunday at Mass he made another announcement. After careful consideration he had decided that the people of the parish shouldn't give up the drink altogether. Instead the quantity produced and drunk was to be reduced by half before Christmas. That way they would have a better chance of adjusting to the new regulations. He'd review the situation again during the following year.

On Christmas Eve the villagers decided to send a bottle of poitín over to Fr. O'Leary to wish him a Happy Christmas and show him they had no hard feelings towards him. They secretly hoped that the priest would take a liking to the drink himself and there would be no more talk about banning it in future. Jack McEvoy, being a wise man and one of the oldest inhabitants of the area, was selected for the job.

"Goodnight Father," said Jack, "I've come to wish you a Happy Christmas on behalf of the people." "That's very kind of you Jack, the same to you and everyone in the parish."
Jack took the bottle out of his pocket and handed it to Fr. O'Leary. "I hope you don't mind, but I've brought you a little present Father. It's just a drop of poitín to warm you up on a cold winter's night."

At first he was going to refuse but on second thoughts he changed his mind.

"Thanks Jack," he said, taking the bottle, "I'll try it. After all, this is the last Christmas there'll be poitín in this parish. With the help of God, by this time next year there won't be a drop to be got."

"Ah sure you'd never know Father, you might be right." replied Jack.

Or maybe, he thought, as he headed up the road for home, with a little help from the Other Man, we might be back in full production.

THERE'S ALWAYS HOPE

Seamus Delaney stood alone on the bridge looking down into the murky water. It was six o'clock on a chilly November morning. It's often said that before a person dies their whole life flashes before their eyes. In Seamus's case, however, this wasn't quite true. He was thinking about his life alright but it wasn't a flash; it was a slower, more drawn-out process. Once he had relived his miserable existence in his head one last time that was it. His mind was made up; there would be no turning back.

His thoughts first wandered back to the days of his childhood. He was one of a large family who lived near a little village in the west of Ireland. Their father was a labourer who worked at all kinds of odd jobs to put food on the table. The trouble was he often mistook the pub for the grocery store and ended up spending his meagre earnings there instead. As soon as they were able the children had to go out and work for local farmers, picking potatoes, weeding turnips and helping with the hay and corn.

Seamus wasn't very bright in school. In those days slow learners received very little encouragement. The schoolmaster never tired of telling him how dense he was, and he spent most of his time in the dunce's corner. He had no luck on the sports field either. Any time he joined in a game of hurling or football he usually ended up doing something stupid and becoming the laughing stock. Eventually he just gave up playing altogether.

When he was fourteen he left school and got a job working on a farm. It was the only kind of work he could expect to do as he could neither read nor write. Over the years his brothers and sisters married and got on with their own lives. He rarely had any contact with them as he felt he had nothing in common with them anymore. The only thing he liked to do was fishing and, when he wasn't working, he spent most of his time on the banks of the river

As the scenes of his life rolled slowly by, he came to the one time when things unexpectedly took a turn for the better. This was when he had met the love of his life, Kathleen.

Kathleen worked behind the counter in Daly's hardware store in the village. The first time he saw her he fell in love with her, but it wasn't until he had purchased several bags of nails, screws and other paraphernalia he had no use for, that he finally plucked up the courage to ask her out, and to his delight she said yes.

For a brief period after that his life took on new meaning. When they had been going out for six months, Seamus was planning to ask her to marry him. Unfortunately he never got the chance. Out of the blue Kathleen told him one night that she wouldn't be seeing him again as she was going to London to work in a big hotel. He wanted to go with her but she said no. She was going to make a fresh start and that included ending her relationship with him.

Seamus was devastated. He couldn't believe that the one person he loved and trusted had turned her back on him, and of course he blamed himself for everything. As time went by he became more and more depressed. Now he had decided he had enough. Nobody would miss him, so what was the point of prolonging this miserable existence of his any longer? A few minutes and it would all be over.

As he stood there shivering with the cold and bracing himself for what he was about to do, suddenly he heard a scream. At first he thought his mind was playing tricks on him, but then he heard it again. It was a woman's voice shouting "Help, Help". He looked around but couldn't see anyone. It was now beginning to get bright and about fifty yards away from the bridge on the narrow country road he could just make out the shape of a house. The voice seemed to be coming from that direction. There must be something terribly wrong, he thought

Without really giving any thought to what he was doing, he left his stand on the bridge and made his way towards the house. When he reached the little gate he could see a woman standing in the doorway

"Hurry, hurry," she called to him, "I need your help."

"What is it? What's wrong?" He asked as he pushed open the gate and hurried up the path to the door.

"It's the baby" she said "It's coming, and I'm here all alone."

Seamus was stunned. What was he supposed to do? He somehow managed to pull himself together and spoke kindly to the woman.

"What do you want me to do?"

"Could you drive me to the hospital?"

"But I don't have a car"

"You can drive my husband's car. I presume you can drive," she said, handing him a bunch of keys.

Seamus helped the woman into the back seat of the car, then started it up and drove out onto the road. Luckily, there was hardly any traffic at that time of the morning so he was able to drive at top speed the whole way to the hospital. He told the woman his name was Seamus and he lived about two miles away. She said her name was Heather. The baby wasn't due for another three weeks. Her husband was away working and wouldn't be back until the following Monday. That was why she was alone in the house. They hadn't expected anything to happen so soon.

"If you hadn't come along when you did I don't know what I would have done."

"I suppose I just happened to be in the right place at the right time."

When they arrived at the hospital he hurried into reception and explained the situation. The hospital staff quickly took control. Now that Heather was being looked after Seamus felt there was no point in him hanging around, so he gave the car keys to the receptionist and left.

After hitching several lifts and walking part of the way, he finally arrived home. He hadn't slept very much during the past few weeks and, after being up all night, he now felt exhausted. He went to bed and to his surprise slept soundly until the following morning. When he awoke he felt better than he had for a long time. For once, his own problems didn't come rushing into his mind; instead he thought about Heather and the events of the previous day. He was glad he had been able to come to her assistance and he hoped that everything would turn out well for her.

One afternoon about three months later Seamus was sitting in the kitchen when he heard a knock on the door. He wondered who it could be as he rarely had visitors. Standing on the doorstep were a young man and woman. The woman had a baby in her arms.

"Hello Seamus," said the woman, smiling, "do you remember me?"

"Oh Yes," he said, recognising her, "you're Heather,

the woman I drove to the hospital one morning."

"That's right. This is my husband, Thomas and I would like to introduce you to our baby daughter, Hope. Do you mind if we come in for a moment?"

"Of course," said Seamus, "I should have invited you in.

Seamus led the way into the kitchen and pulled up two chairs for them to sit on.

"I'm sorry the house is such a mess, but I wasn't expecting visitors."

"Never mind that," said Heather, "we're not here to inspect the house, we're here to thank you for the wonderful favour you did us on the morning that Hope was born."

"Oh there's no need to thank me at all, sure anyone would have done the same."

Heather went on to tell him that the doctors said she had been very lucky to get to the hospital when she did. Another hour and things could have gone very differently; in fact, their baby might not be here with them now. Seamus said he was very happy to have been able to help and he was glad that everything had worked out well for them.

"Before we go," said Thomas, "we want to ask you to do us one more favour."

"Oh, what's that?"

"Well, we are having our daughter christened on Sunday, and we were wondering if you would do us the honour of becoming her godfather? It would mean a lot to us."

Seamus was astounded. He had been all alone in the world for so long; now here he was being asked to take part this intimate family occasion. His first instinct was to say no, but when he looked at the tiny baby asleep in her mother's arms, he hadn't the heart to refuse. After all it wasn't every day he was asked to do something like this.

On the following Sunday, wearing a new suit, Seamus sat in the church with Heather, Thomas and their extended family as the baby was christened and officially given the name Hope. Seamus thought about how his life had suddenly changed for the better. From now on he would always be part of this child's life. No doubt he would experience dark days again, but no matter how bad things were, there would always be Hope.

.

A LIFE OF HIS OWN

His house was quiet on this November evening.
Was it only this morning he had driven his son, Liam,
to the airport and waved goodbye to him as he jetted
off to a new job in that faraway country called Dubai?
To Paul it seemed like a lifetime ago. He been
dreading this day, but now that it had arrived it was
even worse than he had anticipated. How was he
going to fill the weeks and months and maybe even
years ahead?

Paul Ryan who had been a primary teacher all his
life retired five years previously at the age of sixty.
The first three years of his retirement were great. He
was able to spend more time doing all the things he
loved like gardening, D.I.Y., and fishing. His wife,
Kathleen, and he even took a few trips to the West of
Ireland and life was really good. Then two years ago,
after a short illness, Kathleen had passed away. Paul

was heartbroken.

His two daughters who were both working in London came home for the funeral. But when it was over they went back to their own lives across the water. That left only Liam, the youngest, who worked in a bank in the town and was still living at home. This arrangement worked well for a year or so. Liam was happy enough living at home with his father and, of course, Paul was glad of the company. In fact, he often wondered how he would have coped if he'd been left all alone; it wasn't something he liked to think about.

Then one day, out of the blue, Liam announced to his father that he and his girlfriend, Tina, were going to work in Dubai. Paul was shocked. He had always thought of Liam as a bit of a home bird. In the past he never expressed any interest in travelling abroad. He felt sure it was Tina's idea rather than Liam's. She had always seemed rather flighty to him: somebody who could come up with a crazy idea at the drop of a hat. However, his son seemed to have made up his mind so there wasn't really anything Paul could do but wish him luck.

"If things don't work out as planned you know you can always come home."

"Thanks Dad, and if we do decide to stay maybe you can come over for a holiday."

"Maybe," replied Paul doubtfully. He didn't really think there was much chance of that.

As he sat there in the gathering gloom he realised that this would be his first time to spend the night alone in the house since Kathleen and himself had moved in thirty-five years ago. And it wasn't just for one night either; this was something he'd have to get used to. Even though he was feeling sad, suddenly a new idea came to him. I'm going to have to make some changes to my life, he thought. After all I'm only sixty-five years old and in good health. Now that the family have all flown the nest surely there's something useful I can do with the rest of my life. Paul decided the best thing he could do now was have an early night. Tomorrow he could starting thinking about plans for the future.

Over the following days Paul tried to keep busy with all the little jobs that needed to be done around the house and garden. In the evening he'd go for a brisk walk out the quiet country road. Walking helped him to think as he tried to figure out what to do now that he was all alone with so much time on his hands. Perhaps, he thought, he could get a part-time job of some description. However, having worked all his life as a teacher, he didn't really fancy the idea of doing anything else. Maybe he could do some voluntary work. There were always organisations looking for people to help with fund-raising and other activities. He also thought about taking up golf. Perhaps that might be a good way to meet people and get some exercise at the same time.

When Friday night came round he decided to take

a trip down to the pub. Now more than ever he felt the need to get out and hopefully meet some of his cronies for a pint and a chat. When he went in he bought his drink and sat down at a small table near the window. A few minutes later one of his buddies called Timothy came and joined him. After greeting each other and the usual discussion about the weather the conversation gradually came to a halt. Timothy took a drink from his glass and looked at Paul.

"If you don't mind me saying so, you seem a bit down tonight, is there anything wrong?"

"No, there's nothing wrong. It's just that Liam left for Dubai on Monday, and I'm trying to adjust to the idea of living on my own for the first time in my life."

"That will take some getting used to alright. Have you any plans?"

"No, I've been considering a few possibilities, that's all."

Paul briefly went through the different options he'd been thinking about during the week. Then there was silence for a while as the two men sat there companionably sipping their pints. Timothy was the first to speak.

"Have you ever thought about travelling?

"Travelling?"

"Yes, I have a great idea. Do you want to hear it?"

"Ok, go on. I suppose it can't do any harm anyway."

"Well, you mentioned volunteering as something you might like to do. Why don't you go a step further and volunteer abroad?"

"Oh, I don't know about that. Where would I go or what would I do?"

"You could go to almost any part of the world you choose. So many developing countries are crying out for teachers, with your experience you'd be an ideal candidate.

"How do you know so much about this?"

"The wife's cousin who is about your age spent last year in Peru working as a teacher with a volunteer organisation. He did loads of travelling and sight-seeing in his free time. In fact, he enjoyed it so much he's planning on going somewhere entirely different next year."

"That sounds interesting alright. I'll definitely think about it."

"Don't just think about it. Go on the internet and you'll find all the information you need."

"Aye, sure I suppose there's nothing that can't be googled nowadays."

When Paul went home that night he was still thinking about Timothy's suggestion. He had to admit that the idea appealed to him, but at the same time he wondered if he'd be foolish to go gallivanting around the world at his age. After all, he had very little experience of travelling in the past. All his holidays had been spent in Ireland except for that one time when Kathleen and himself went on a two week package holiday to the Canary Islands. Everything had been organised for them, flights, taxis, hotel and daytrips. All they had to do was relax and enjoy themselves. He realised that this would be a completely different ball game. For one thing, he wouldn't have his beloved Kathleen with him. He'd be landing himself in a completely different culture where he'd probably have to learn a new language and get to know the local people.

Over the following days, even though he told himself to forget all about the idea, he couldn't stop thinking about it. In the end curiosity got the better of him and he fired up the laptop. There's no harm in getting some information, he thought; it doesn't mean I have to do anything about it. He wasn't long searching when he found a website specialising in volunteering abroad for retired teachers. They were looking for people in several parts of the world including Asia, Africa and South America for periods from three months up to two years. There were several pictures of volunteers working with school children in some of the poorest parts of the world.

After reading through all the information he came to a decision. He opened up the online application form, carefully filled in the required details and, without giving himself time to change his mind, pressed the *send* button. So far so good, he thought. Now I'll just have to wait and see if I get a response. He didn't have long to wait. The following day somebody from the voluntary organisation sent him an email thanking him for his application and asking if they could contact him by phone. He replied confirming a date and time for the call.

As he sat there waiting for the phone to ring Paul felt rather nervous, but he needn't have worried. The lady who rang him called Angela was very friendly and answered any questions he had.

"Have you any idea where you'd like to go?" she asked.

"No, I haven't made up my mind yet, can I take some time to think about it".

"Of course you can, take as long as you like. I'll send you on our online brochure which will explain everything in detail. When you've decided which country you want to go to send me an email and we'll take it from there."

Even though he studied the brochure several times over, in the days that followed, Paul still couldn't make up his mind where he wanted to go. Every country he read about had something different to recommend it. He wished he could go to them all but, of course, he knew that wasn't possible. In the end the decision was taken out of his hands. He received an email from Angela asking if she could arrange another phone call to which he agreed.

"I have a proposition for you." said Angela.

"Oh, what sort of proposition?"

"Well, the thing is we're looking for a teacher for Guatemala in Central America in two weeks time. The person we had for the position had to cancel due to illness. We're just wondering if you'd be interested. If not, there's no problem, you can take your time and decide where you want to go."

Paul's brain was trying hard to process what he had just heard. Guatemala, in two weeks time, he thought, could it be possible?

"Are you still there?" asked Angela when there was no reply from him.

"Sorry, I was just wondering if I heard you correctly. So it's Guatemala, in two weeks. How long is the contract for?"

"Well initially, it's for three months, but if everything goes well and you want to stay longer there'll be no problem. What do you think?"

"I'll go!" replied Paul without hesitation.

"Are you sure you don't want to think about it and get back to me?"

"No, I'm certain. I've been poring over that brochure you sent me and I was getting nowhere nearer to making a decision. Now the decision has been made for me. Call it fate or whatever you like, but I think this is the best thing that could have happened."

Over the next two weeks Paul was busy getting everything organised. His sister, Nora, who lived not too far away agreed to look after the house while he was away. He was going to contact his children to let him know his plans, but then he changed his mind. If I let them know now, he thought, they'll think their old dad has finally lost his marbles and try to persuade me not to go. I'll wait until I arrive at my destination; then there's nothing they can do about it.

Two weeks later Paul was in Heathrow Airport waiting for a connecting flight to Guatemala when his phone beeped. When he looked at it he saw that it was a message from Liam which read:

Hi Dad,
Hope this finds you well. Things haven't worked out as planned here. Tina is staying, but I'm going home. Could you meet me tomorrow at Dublin Airport at 5 pm? Thanks a lot, Liam.

Finding a seat Paul sat down, took a deep breath and replied to the text:

Hi Liam,
Sorry to hear that things haven't worked out. I'm afraid I won't be able to meet you at the airport tomorrow. I'm on my way to a teaching position in Guatemala for three months, maybe longer. You'll have to get the bus home. You can call to your Auntie Nora for the key. I'll contact you when I get to my destination and explain everything, your loving Dad.

A couple of minutes later his phone beeped again. This time he read:

Hi Dad,
Is this a joke or have you finally taken leave of your senses? How could you make a decision like that without contacting your family first? And another thing, how am I going to manage on my own in the house? You know I've never used the cooker, washing machine or dishwasher in my life. This is a disaster if ever there was one, Liam.

Paul wrote back:

Hi Liam,
Don't worry about using the kitchen appliances. All the
instruction manuals are in the top drawer in the kitchen
cupboard. A smart young lad like you should have no bother
figuring it all out. I have to go now as the plane is boarding.
Talk to you soon, Love Dad.

As Paul made his way onto the plane with the rest of the passengers, there was a spring in his step that hadn't been there in a long time. He was ready for whatever lay ahead, and he was pretty sure he'd have no regrets.

THE BABY BROTHER

Shortly after three o'clock in the afternoon Mrs Moran was finishing her cup of tea when she heard the bell ring.   Hurrying out to the shop she greeted her first two after-school customers of the day, Maggie and Annie O'Brien.

"Hello Girls and how was school today?"

"Ok"

"I suppose it's the usual for you two?"

"Yes, please."

The two girls dug deep in the pockets of their well worn school dresses and each produced a penny which they placed on the counter. Mrs Moran took down one of the big glass jars from the shelf, unscrewed the lid and handed the children a lollipop each. Suddenly the door swung open and in came the third after-school customer, Joanne Buckley.

"What can I get you Joanne," ask Mrs Moran as

she returned the jar of lollipops to the shelf.
"I'll have a sixpenny ice-cream, please." replied Joanne placing a shiny sixpenny piece on the counter.

In those days, in the nineteen-sixties, a sixpenny ice-cream was every child's dream. It consisted of a delicious slice of vanilla ice-cream wedged between two wafers. They were usually reserved for special occasions, and for Maggie and Annie those occasions were very rare indeed. However, Joanne who was an only child never seemed to have a shortage of pocket money. In fact, she could have a sixpenny ice-cream every day if she wanted, and she usually did. When they all went outside she licked the ice-cream while the others looked on longingly. "Enjoy your lollipops" she smirked as she hopped on her bicycle and cycled away.

Maggie who was eleven and Annie who was eight lived with their parents, John and Mary, in a small cottage about a mile from the village. Mary was a good wife and mother who looked after her family as best she could. When they were first married her husband had a steady job with a builder and they were all well provided for. Then, for some reason, he started spending a lot of his time in the pub, which was something he had never done in his younger days, and eventually he lost his job. Now he only worked on days when he felt like it. The rest of the time was either spent in the pub or sleeping off the effects of the night before.

Mary often tried to talk to her husband about his

drinking but he refused to listen. Despite her best efforts to keep things as normal as possible the whole family were affected by his behaviour. After paying the rent and putting food on the table there was very little money for anything else. The girls rarely got new clothes and had to attend school in their old patched dresses and shoes that had seen better days. They hated having to go to school dressed like paupers. Most of the other children were kind, but there were a few who laughed and made fun of them. After a while they grew accustomed to being the poorest children in the school. It seemed to them that nothing would ever change; they'd always be in the ha'penny place.

But then a few weeks later something did happen which would surely change their lives. Their mother told them that they were soon going to have a new baby brother or sister. The two girls looked at her in astonishment.

"But are we not too old to get a new baby?" ask Annie, "Maggie's eleven and I'm eight. Won't the baby be tiny compared to us?"

"That's true," agreed their mother, "but it also means that the two of you will be able to help me to look after it."

"Really?" asked Maggie incredulously, "you'll let us help look after it?"

"Of course I will, sure I'll be glad of all the help I can get."

The two girls were delighted. This was the best

news they had ever heard. As far as they knew none of the children in their classes at school had a baby brother or sister. Now at long last they'd have something to be proud of.

A few months later their mother was taken by ambulance to the hospital twenty miles away to get the new baby while their father looked after them at home. After three days Mrs. Mulhern their nearest neighbour who had a telephone in the house came puffing and panting up the road.

"They're after ringing from the hospital. Your wife had a baby boy a couple of hours ago. Mother and baby are doing fine. Congratulations!"

There was great excitement in the house when Mary arrived home with the new baby. After a lot of discussion they decided to call him Seán after his father. John was so proud of his son. In fact, from that day on he gave up drinking and started working every hour he could to provide for his family.

Maggie and Annie too were besotted by the new baby. They did everything they could to help their mother to look after him, and never tired of talking about him in school. They didn't care now whether their clothes were patched or worn. Those things didn't matter anymore. They had a baby brother called Seán who was the most beautiful baby in the whole wide world.

Then one day when he was six months old Mary allowed them to take him to the shop in his pram. Maggie went in to get some messages for their mother while Annie stayed outside with the baby. When Maggie came out they sat down on an old stone seat outside the shop before heading for home. They were only there a few minutes when down the road on her bicycle came Joanne Buckley. They couldn't believe their luck; this was what they'd been hoping for. She hurried into the shop and came back out a few minutes later with her big sixpenny ice-cream in her hand. She looked first at the two girls sitting on the seat and then at the baby in his pram.

"Who owns the baby?" she asked.

"We do," replied Maggie proudly.

"You needn't look so smug. Anyone would think he was the only baby in the world," said Joanne.

Annie got up from where she was sitting and walked over to Joanne. Drawing herself up to her full height and looking her directly in the eye, she declared:

"Well, I'll tell you one thing Joanne Buckley, he's better than an old sixpenny ice-cream any day!"

Without another word the two girls turned and walked proudly down the road pushing the pram with its precious cargo, while Joanne stood staring open-mouthed after them.

TIME TO MOVE ON

Ellie O'Brien used her apron to wipe the sweat from her forehead.   It was a beautiful sunny day in June nineteen-fifty. However, she didn't have much time to enjoy or even notice the weather. She had spent the entire morning scrubbing clothes on the big washboard and was now hanging them out on the line. At least they'll be dry in a couple of hours, she thought, and then I can bring them in and get on with the ironing.

Nineteen year old Ellie was employed by Mr and Mrs Johnston who were the wealthy owners of a large house and estate about a mile outside the town. The house was known locally as "The Big House". The estate consisted of a farm and stables where they bred racehorses. Up to ten men were employed on the estate at any given time while inside in the house there were three women. In top position was Mrs

Dawson; a middle-aged woman who did all the cooking. Next came Nora who was Mrs Dawson's assistant, helping in the kitchen and serving meals. On the bottom rung of the ladder was Ellie who was given all the back-breaking jobs that nobody else wanted to do.

As she was picking up her basket to return to the house a car sped up the avenue and into the yard. The passenger door opened and a young man jumped out. He took a suitcase from the back seat and waved to the driver who immediately drove out the gate and back down the avenue.

"Hello there," he smiled at Ellie as she came across the yard with the basket under her arm. "Isn't it a beautiful day?"

"Is it? I hadn't time to notice, I've been working hard all morning."

The young man was amused by her answer. "If you don't mind me asking," he continued, "What's your name?"

"I'm Ellie O'Brien. I've been working here for the past three months. And who are you?"

"I'm David, the youngest member of the Johnston family. I'm the one who's studying to be a doctor."

"Oh, that's great," replied Ellie without much enthusiasm.

"What's even better is that today is the start of my summer holidays. For the next two months I can do exactly what I please: two whole months of freedom. Isn't it fantastic?"

He seemed so happy that Ellie couldn't help smiling. "It is indeed. Well if you don't mind I have work to do."

"Ok, I'm sure I'll see you around," he picked up his suitcase and strolled casually towards the house.

That night when she was alone in her little room Ellie found herself thinking about David. She couldn't believe how friendly he had been towards her. His two older brothers who helped run the estate never spoke to her except when they wanted something done. But David was different. As she drifted off to sleep she couldn't help wondering when she'd get the chance to talk to him again

Over the following weeks they saw each other often and became good friends. Then one day when they were alone he kissed her and asked her if she'd be his girlfriend. Ellie was thrilled. She had never had a boyfriend before and she really liked David.

"There is only one thing," he said, "we'll have to keep our relationship a secret."

"Why is that?" asked Ellie.

"Because we're too young," answered David.

However, this wasn't true. It wasn't their ages he was worried about. He knew that if his parents found out he was seeing one of the servants he'd be in big trouble.

Most evenings when her work was finished Ellie would sneak out to meet David. They would meet well away from the house and go for a walk in the woods or down by the river. Everything was going great for while. Then disaster struck. One evening, when they were both feeling particularly romantic towards each other, they threw caution to the wind and ended up making love. A few weeks later Emily discovered she was pregnant. She couldn't believe she had been so stupid to let this happen. What was she going to do? When she broke the news to David the colour drained from his face. She thought he was going to collapse.

"Well," she said, "say something."

"I don't know what to say" he mumbled.

"Well you could say you love me, and everything is going to be alright."

"I do love you Ellie, but... but my parents will go berserk when they find out."

His parents' reaction was as bad as he expected.

"What were you thinking of?" demanded his mother. We're sending you to one of the best colleges in the country and you have a bright future ahead of you. Yet this is how you repay us – by carrying on with one of the maids."

"But I love her and I want to marry her."

"You can forget about that," growled his father, "no son of mine is going to marry a servant girl."

"But what'll happen to Ellie?"

"Don't worry about her" replied his father, "we'll take care of everything. All you have to do is concentrate on returning to college next week, or is that too much to ask?"

"No" replied David weakly.

After that everything happened quickly. The Johnstons sent for Ellie's father who lived in a small village about ten miles away. They told him what had happened trying to make it sound like it was all Ellie's fault; they said she had thrown herself at him. Finally, they offered them a sum of one hundred pounds on condition that Ellie would be sent away and nobody in the locality would ever know what happened. The good name of the Johnston family had to be preserved at all costs. Both Ellie and her father knew that they had no choice but to take the money and leave. Ellie realised that she had made a terrible mistake getting involved with someone from a different social class. However, she still couldn't bring herself to think badly of David. She believed that he did love her. He was just too weak to stand up to his parents and now she was going to suffer the consequences. So she gathered up her few belongings and left with her father that evening. She never saw David again.

A week later it was David's turn to pack his suitcase and go back to college where he was starting his second year. His parents were glad to see him go. Surely now, they thought, he'll forget all about Ellie and get on with his studies. He had achieved top grades in his first year exams and they expected no less from him in the second year. After a couple of months, however, David knew he wasn't doing as well as he should be. He had difficulty concentrating during lectures and he often found his mind wandering off. He couldn't stop thinking of Ellie and feeling guilty about what had happened. David had never been fond of drink but now he found that alcohol helped him to forget his worries. Instead of studying, as he should have been, he idled his time away in the bars.

As a result of all this, David ended up failing his exams at the end of the year. His parents were extremely disappointed. They had such high hopes of him becoming a doctor. He told them he wanted to give up college altogether but they wouldn't hear of it. So after a lot of persuasion he went back to repeat the year. This time, however, it was even more disastrous than before. Half way through the year the college authorities advised him to give it up. There was no point in continuing to waste everyone's time and his parents' money. And so ended the dream of the Johnstons' youngest son becoming a doctor.

Unfortunately, his troubles didn't end there. Despite the best efforts of his parents to get him involved in the running of the estate, his life just seemed to have taken on a downhill spiral from which there was no return. Eventually they had to be satisfied with giving him odd jobs to do around the farm. As soon as he got paid he'd head straight for the pub and wouldn't leave until all the money was gone. Then he'd make his way home to sleep off the effects of his drinking spree and the cycle would start all over again.

The people in the village became used to seeing

David Johnston from the "Big House" squander his money and his life away in the pub. They felt sorry for him. He was a likeable young man who never did any harm to anyone but himself. They simply wondered what made someone, with such a promising career ahead of him, end up a hopeless alcoholic. Of course there were several rumours but nobody only David and his family knew the real cause of his distress.

One evening at about seven o'clock he was sitting alone at the bar in Tom McGraths pub with the first pint of the night in front of him. Tom was busy tidying the bar as he got ready for the night's business. Suddenly David spoke.

"I've made up my mind, Tom; I'm going to look for her."

Tom stopped what he was doing and looked quizzically at him. He had no idea who he was talking about. "Look for who, David?" he asked.

"I'm going to look for Ellie"

"Who's Ellie? Is she someone you knew at college?"

David didn't answer, just stared at the pint in front of him on the counter. Tom felt sorry for the young man. He knew that something had been troubling him for a long time and he wondered if he could help.

"Well, if you feel like talking, I'm willing to listen, and you can be sure that anything you say to me won't go any further. I've never betrayed a confidence yet and I'm not going to start now."

David knew this was true. Tom wasn't the type to

gossip about his customers as soon as they turned their backs, so he ended up telling him the whole story from beginning to end.

"That's a sad story indeed," said Tom, "I'm sorry things turned out the way they did. But are you sure that going to look for her now is a good idea? She's probably built a new life for herself and you turning up out of the blue might just cause her more upset. Is that what you really want?"

"No, but what else can I do? I certainly can't carry on like this much longer. The guilt is eating me up. I just need to find out if she's ok. If I could talk to her and tell her how sorry I am, maybe I could put it behind me and move on."

"Well, don't do anything hasty. Think about it for a few days and let me know what you decide."

After talking to Tom about his dilemma David was more determined than ever to find Ellie. He got in touch with an old school friend of her's who reluctantly gave him some information. He discovered that when Ellie had left his parents' house she had gone to stay with her married sister who lived in a small town about fifty miles away. She had a baby boy whom she called Thomas. Two years later she married a local man and they had two more children.

It was a bit of a shock to David to hear that Ellie was married, but he was still determined to go see her. All he needed now was her address. At first Ellie's friend refused to tell him where she lived, but after much persuasion she gave in and wrote down the address on a piece of paper and gave it to him. Now he had all the information he needed.

The following day he went into the pub to see Tom again and told him what he had found out about Ellie.

"Well, are you still thinking of visiting her?" asked Tom.

"I certainly am and I even found out where she lives." David took the address out of his pocket and handed it to Tom. "The only problem is I don't know how I'm going to get there."

Tom studied the address for a moment. "I still don't know if it's such a good idea, but if you're really determined to go see her I'll drive you there myself."

"Thanks Tom, that's very kind of you."

A few days later David and Tom set off on their journey. David was very quiet on the way and Tom wondered what he was thinking. By the time they got to the town where Ellie lived it was getting dark. After driving around for a while they eventually found the housing estate named on the piece of paper. Tom stopped the car and David got out. He made his way slowly along the pavement until he came to number twenty-seven, opened the little gate and walked up the path. He was just about to knock on the door when he happened to glance at the window to his right. There was a white lace curtain covering the window, but he noticed that the bottom corner was pulled back slightly leaving a tiny part of the glass visible.

Instead of knocking on the door as he had planned he went over to the window and peeped in taking care not to be seen by anyone inside.

What he saw was a cosy living-room with a cheery fire burning in an open fireplace. Ellie and her husband sat in armchairs on either side. The three children were seated at a table with copybooks and pencils and seemed to be engrossed in what they were doing. The whole picture was one of peace and contentment. As he stood there taking in the scene a strange feeling came over him. He knew that Tom was right. Ellie had made a new life for herself and her son. The last thing she'd want now was for him to turn up out of the blue. Hadn't he caused her enough pain and grief already? The best thing he could do now, he realised, was to turn around and walk away. So without another moment's hesitation he left the house and made his way back to the car.

"Well, how did it go?" asked Tom as David opened the door and got into the passenger seat. "I didn't go in," he said, telling Tom what he had seen. "It was only when I saw them all sitting there together, looking so happy and contented, that I realised the best thing I could do was let them get on with their lives."

"I think you made the right decision," replied Tom "and you won't regret it."

Over the days and weeks that followed David began to look at things in a new light. Now that he had seen for himself that Ellie and Thomas were getting on with their lives, maybe it was time for him to try to get his own life back on track too. If his son ever came looking for him he would be there. Otherwise, all he could do was to leave them in peace and wish them all the happiness they deserved.

THE DOCTOR'S DILEMMA

Shortly after one o'clock in the morning Dr Cornelius Maher and his wife Mabel were asleep when the telephone rang downstairs in the hallway. Cornelius was dead to the world, so there was no chance of him hearing it. At first Mabel thought she was dreaming, but slowly she realised it was real. She knew her husband wasn't capable of answering the phone, not in his condition, so she decided to go down and answer it herself.

"Hello, how can I help you?" she asked.

"This is Frank Dwyer here. Can I speak to Dr Maher?" said a man's voice.

"I'm afraid Dr Maher can't come to the phone, he isn't well."

"What do you mean, he isn't well? This is an

emergency."

"What sort of emergency, Mr Dwyer?"

"My wife is having a baby. It's not due for a few weeks but looks like it has decided to come early."

"I'm sorry, but my husband has been extremely unwell all day, so he won't be able to go to your assistance.

"What are we going to do? We have to get a doctor somewhere."

She could hear the panic in his voice. "I'll give you the phone number for Dr O'Callaghan. I'm sure he'll be able to look after your wife."

Mabel gave the number to Frank Dwyer, hung up the phone and went back to bed. She felt terrible about lying on behalf of her husband. Cornelius wasn't sick; he was the worse for wear after drinking too much alcohol that evening. They had gone out to the local hotel for dinner with some friends they hadn't seen in a long time. One thing led to another and Cornelius ended up drinking far more than he could handle. In fact, he was so drunk they ended up having to leave the car at the hotel and got a taxi home. He should have been on duty tonight for emergency calls. She hoped Dr O'Callaghan would be able to look after the Dwyers; otherwise there might be severe repercussions for her husband.

Dr John O'Callaghan was in his seventies and lived in the next village about three miles away. He had retired some years previously but still did a little part-time work and had just a few private patients. When he asked Frank Dwyer why his own doctor couldn't do the call, Frank told him that Dr Maher's wife had said he was sick. Realising it was an emergency and there was nobody else available, Dr O'Callaghan agreed to go. However, he had no idea where Dwyers lived so Frank had to give him directions over the phone.

"Can you please hurry Doctor," begged Frank, "There's no time to spare."

"Try not to worry; I'll be there as quick as I can."

Despite his best efforts to follow the directions he'd been given, somewhere along the way he took a wrong turn which brought him miles out of his way. As a result, it took him much longer to reach the Dwyer house than it should have. When he got there the baby, a little boy, had already been born. A neighbouring woman who had no experience of childbirth was doing her best to look after Mrs Dwyer and the baby until the doctor arrived. The baby seemed to be fine but Mrs Dwyer wasn't doing so well. The doctor did what he could for her and instructed her husband to call an ambulance without delay. Sadly, about an hour later before the ambulance arrived, Mrs Dwyer passed away.

As Dr O'Callaghan drove home a couple of hours later he felt extremely sorry for Frank Dwyer who now had to face the prospect of rearing four children without his spouse. In the first place, it was so unfortunate that Dr Maher had been too sick to attend the birth. Secondly, if he hadn't lost his way and got there earlier, would things have been different? Sadly, now they'd never know.

At ten o'clock the following morning Dr O'Callaghan decided he had better phone Cornelius Maher to break the bad news to him about the death of his patient the previous night. Cornelius who just got out of bed answered the phone.

"Hello Cornelius, John O'Callaghan here."

"Good morning John."

"I hope I'm not disturbing you. I believe you were very sick yesterday. Are you feeling any better this morning?"

"Who told you I was sick?"

"Frank Dwyer. When he rang your house looking for you last night, Mabel said you were very sick and you wouldn't be able to attend his wife"

"Oh yes," said Cornelius, laughing. "She told him I was sick. She couldn't very well say I was sleeping off the effects of too much alcohol, now could she?"

John wondered if he had heard correctly. "Are you saying the reason you couldn't attend Mrs Dwyer last night was that you were drunk?"

"Don't sound so shocked John. I'm sure you often had a few too many yourself when you weren't supposed to. How did you get on anyway, did everything go smoothly?"

"No, I'm afraid it didn't. I took a wrong turn on the way there with the result that I was late arriving. The baby had already been born when I got there. He was ok, but his mother wasn't. The poor woman died an hour later."

Cornelius was stunned at this news. He couldn't believe that somebody had died, probably as a result of his negligence. However, his biggest concern at that moment was that he had already told John that he had been drunk the night before. There was silence on the line for a few moments; then Cornelius spoke.

"What are you going to do John?" he asked nervously, "are you going to inform the authorities?" "I don't know," replied John, "I need time to think. Call in to see me tomorrow; we'll talk about it then."

At first John was pretty sure he was going to report Cornelius's behaviour to the authorities. This was a very serious matter. If he didn't, maybe the same thing would happen again in the future. However, when Cornelius called to see him he was in such a state that John felt sorry for him. Cornelius begged him for a second chance and swore that nothing like that would ever happen again. In the end, John agreed to back up his story that he was sick instead of being under the influence of alcohol, thus enabling Dr Cornelius Maher to continue working as a general practitioner as if nothing had happened.

Meanwhile, the Dwyer family had no choice but to get on with their lives without their mother. The baby was christened Stephen and the whole family doted on him. Frank's sister, Kitty, who wasn't married, moved in to help with the children. They were very lucky to have her, and in time she became almost like a second mother to them. The three older children weren't fond of school and left as soon as they could. After working in dead end jobs locally for a couple of years, one by one they emigrated to England, lured by the promise of higher pay and a better standard of living.

Stephen, however, was different. He was an extremely bright student who loved school. When he completed his Leaving Certificate obtaining top marks in his class, his family couldn't have been prouder. Shortly afterwards he got a job in the office of a large manufacturing company in the nearby town. This was considered quite a good position in those days of the nineteen-sixties, and his father was relieved that at least one of his children wouldn't have to take the boat to England to earn a decent living.

Stephen was happy to get the job and enjoyed working with his new colleagues. However, this wasn't his dream job. When he was seven years old, his father told about how his mother had died the night he was born. His father assured him it wasn't his fault, but secretly he couldn't help thinking that maybe he was somehow to blame. Over time he came to a decision: when he grew up he'd be a doctor! In that way he reckoned he'd be able to help other people and maybe prevent a similar tragedy from happening to someone else. Whenever anybody asked him what he was going to be when he grew up, his answer was always the same: "I'm going to be a doctor".

As he got older, however, he realised that, in all

likelihood, he'd never achieve his dream. In those days the education system was very different from what it is today. Going to university didn't just require brains; it also required money, and lots of it. Therefore, it was unrealistic for someone like Stephen from a working-class background to even think of becoming a doctor. However, even though he didn't talk about his dream anymore, that didn't stop him from secretly keeping it close to his heart.

Dr Cornelius Maher continued to live in the area, but had no more contact with the Dwyer family after Stephen was born. They now attended a new doctor who had recently moved into the district and lived closer to their home. He heard that the baby had been christened Stephen but that was all he knew about him. Cornelius was so relieved that Dr O'Callaghan hadn't reported him that he gave up drinking altogether and became more conscientious about his work. However, as time went by he couldn't help feeling guilty about the death of Mrs Dwyer, and he often wished he had owned up to his actions and accepted the consequences at the time. Dr Maher and his wife were by now quite well to do, and they had no family of their own to spend their money on. Every now and again he'd think that perhaps he should make a financial donation to the Dwyer family as some sort of compensation, but he never got around to doing anything about it.

Then, one frosty morning in January Cornelius left his home early to drive to the clinic in the village. As he rounded a sharp bend the car went out of control and skidded headlong into a stone wall. The first to arrive on the scene was Stephen Dwyer who was on his way to work. He found Dr Maher slumped unconsciously over the steering wheel. Even though he didn't know Dr Maher personally, he recognised him as a doctor who lived locally. Hurrying to the phone box in the village, he called an ambulance, and the doctor was rushed to the nearest hospital. Cornelius regained consciousness later in the day to find that he had a broken arm along with some cuts and bruises to his head and face. Of course he couldn't remember anything that happened after the accident, so he asked one of the nurses if she knew who had called the ambulance for him. She went to reception to find out.

"The Good Samaritan was a young man called Stephen Dwyer. He was driving to work and was the first person to arrive on the scene."

Cornelius felt drowsy from all the medication but even so the name registered immediately. What a co-incidence it was, he thought, that Stephen Dwyer should be the one to help him in his hour of need. A few days later when he was feeling better, he sent a message to Stephen asking him to call in to see him in the hospital.

"Hello Stephen, thanks for coming in, won't you take a seat." said Cornelius, pointing to the chair beside the bed.

"Thanks Doctor, how are you feeling? I hope you're

on the mend."

"I am indeed, I'm feeling much better. I'd like to thank you for calling the ambulance the other morning. If you hadn't come along God only knows how long I would have been there for. There isn't much traffic at that time of morning. Oh, and by the way, there's no need to call me Doctor, Cornelius will do fine."

"There's no need to thank me at all, I'm just glad that I happened to be in the right place at the right time."

"You're Stephen Dwyer, Frank's youngest son, isn't that right?"

The two of them chatted for a while and Cornelius asked Stephen where he was working. On hearing about his new job in the office of a manufacturing company, he enquired if Stephen liked working there.

"It's alright for the moment, but it's not what I really want to do."

Cornelius was interested. "If you had your choice then," he asked," what would your dream job be?"

"You might find this hard to believe, but I've always wanted to be a doctor"

Stephen explained that even though his Leaving Cert results were good enough to get him a place in medical school it was no use, because his father just didn't have the money to put him through college.

"I'm going to work for a few years and try to save enough money for college. I don't even know if I'll manage to do that, but it's the only hope I have."

Before Stephen left the hospital that day,

Cornelius had already come to a decision: he would pay for Stephen's education in medical school thus enabling him to realise his dream. He'd just have to run it past Mabel first, but he felt sure she'd have no objection.

A few weeks later when Cornelius was back on his feet again he called to Dwyers house to talk to Stephen and his father. They were taken aback by his proposal.

"But why would you want to do something like that?" asked Frank, "I know Stephen called the ambulance that morning when you had the accident. But paying his way through college, it just seems too much. We couldn't expect that of you."

"You'd be doing me a favour by accepting," replied Cornelius, "as you know, Mabel and I have no family of our own and nothing would make us happier than getting the opportunity to pay for Stephen's education – especially as he wants to become a doctor."

In the end they agreed to accept Dr Maher's generous offer and Stephen started college the following September. Cornelius and Mabel were guests of honour at his graduation five years later. As he posed for a photo with Stephen in the college grounds the sun suddenly peeped out from behind a cloud and he couldn't help feeling that Mrs Dwyer was looking down with pride at her son. Maybe now, he thought, is a good time to put the past firmly behind us, as we all look forward to a brighter future.

THE ANGEL

It was the last week in July. James Conlan was busy mending the fences around his few acres of stony land; it was that time of year again. He would soon be making the journey from his home in the west of Ireland to the big farm in County Meath where he worked for three months every year during the harvest. He considered himself very lucky to have the job. It helped him to clothe and feed his family which consisted of five children, four girls and a boy. Without it he would have found it very difficult to make a living from his own few acres.

As he hammered a nail into the post to secure the wire he looked up and saw his seven year old son Tommy crossing the field.

"Hello Tommy," he said, "have you come to

help?"

"To tell you the truth Dad I had to get out of the house for a while, listening to all those women would drive a man to distraction. What do you want me to do?"

James smiled at his son. He was used to him complaining about being surrounded by women. He sometimes wished Tommy had a brother but seemingly that wasn't to be. He soon found him something to do and the two of them worked away amicably in the warm afternoon sunshine. After a while Tommy spoke.

"Dad, there's something I want to ask you."
"What?" asked James, not taking much notice but continuing with what he was doing.
"I was wondering if I could go with you this year."
"Go where with me?"
"To County Meath, when you go to work there for the harvest."
"I'm afraid not Tommy. Sure the work is hard and the hours are long. I wouldn't have time to look after you. It'd be no place for a seven year old boy."
"Please Dad, I wouldn't be any trouble at all and maybe I could help out around the farm."
"Oh, I don't know Tommy. I'll tell you what; I'll talk to your mother about it tonight and see what she has to say. But I'm not making any promises, mind.
Tommy's face broke into a huge smile. "Thanks Dad," he said and went back to the job he was doing.

Later that night when the children were all in bed

James asked his wife, Sheila, about Tommy's request. She told him in no uncertain terms what she thought.

"It's the most ludicrous idea I ever heard in all my life."

"Well I thought that at first too, but the more I think about it, the more it seems to make sense. You know how Tommy is always complaining about being surrounded by girls. Maybe it'd do him good to get away for a couple of months. Wouldn't it be a bit of a holiday for him? And sure if he was really homesick I could bring him home early and go back myself."

After a lot of persuasion Tommy's mother agreed to let him go. When they told Tommy the following day he was thrilled; he felt so grown up, going off to work with his father for the harvest.

A week later they were ready to leave. Their journey began with a three mile walk to the nearest town. From there they caught a bus to County Meath. When they arrived in Meath they were met by the farmer, Mr Smith, who drove them to the farm in a battered old van. Tommy was amazed by the size of the farmhouse and surrounding buildings; it was so big compared to their own place at home.

Their sleeping quarters consisted of a converted barn which they shared with three other farm hands who had come from different parts of the country. At first Tommy thought it a bit strange to be sleeping in an outhouse but he wasn't long getting used to the idea and he slept like a log that night.

The crowing of the rooster woke Tommy early the

following morning. At first everything looked strange and he couldn't figure out where he was; he thought he must be dreaming. But then it all came back to him. He sat up in his bed and looked around. His father and the other workers were still fast asleep. At home he was used to getting up early so he sneaked out of bed, put on his clothes and went out into the yard. It was a beautiful morning and the sun was just coming up.

He wandered around the yard for some time taking in his new surroundings. Then he opened the little gate and went out into a haggard at the back of the house. Down at the end of the haggard he was surprised to see the farmer's wife, Mrs Smith, sitting on a large flat stone. All around her a flock of hens pecked vigorously at the food she was throwing to them. He thought she looked rather forlorn sitting there all on her own at that hour of the morning. When she saw him approaching, however, Mrs Smith smiled at him and asked him if he had slept well. When she had finished feeding the hens she invited him into the kitchen for some breakfast.

Tommy didn't like to refuse so he followed her rather timidly into the kitchen. As soon as he got inside he could feel the heat from the range. A shaggy old sheepdog lying in the corner opened one eye and winked at him, then when back to sleep again. Mrs Smith bade him sit on a long form which ran the length of a well scrubbed wooden table. Tommy did as he was told and it wasn't long until he had a bowl of steaming hot porridge in front of him.

"Get that inside you now," she said, "it'll make you big and strong."

As he sat there eating the porridge a thought suddenly struck him.

"Where are your children, Mrs Smith?" he asked, "are they still in bed?"

"No," she answered, busying herself at the range, "we don't have any children."

Tommy thought this was very strange. He lived in a small house and his parents had five children. How could Mr and Mrs Smith live in a big house like this and have no children? It made no sense at all. Surely the bigger the house people lived in, the more children they'd have.

After that there was silence for a while. Tommy continued to eat his porridge while his eyes wandered around the kitchen. Presently his gaze fell on a small white object which stood on the mantelpiece over the fireplace. He stared at it, trying to figure out what it was, until his curiosity got the better of him.

"What's that?" he asked, pointing to the object.

"It's an angel," replied Mrs Smith.

"And who does it belong to?"

"It belongs to my little boy."

Tommy was confused. "But you said you don't have any children."

Mrs Smith came over to the table and sat down opposite him.

"It's true, we don't have any children now, but we

did at one time have a little boy called Daniel. He died when he was a year old. He'd be six now if he had lived. What age are you Tommy?"

"I'm seven."

"There you are now," she smiled, "maybe you can think of him as your little brother."

Tommy thought this was a good idea; since he was an only boy it would be nice to think of Daniel as his little brother - even if he was in heaven.

"And the angel belonged to Daniel?"

"Yes, his grandfather made it for him shortly after he was born. I have to take care of it for him now. In fact," she added sadly, "it's almost the only thing I have left belonging to him."

Suddenly Mrs Smith looked at the clock. "It's seven o'clock; the men will be getting up. You better go back out to your father or he'll think you're gone missing." Tommy thanked Mrs Smith for the porridge and hurried back out to the barn.

From that day on things started to get really busy on the farm. There was so much to be done. First the corn had to be cut with a scythe and tied into sheaves. The sheaves were built into stooks and later stacks to dry out. When it was dry it was brought into the haggard and made into a big reek ready for threshing. Tommy enjoyed spending the days in the field with his father. He'd work for a couple of hours then lie down on the headland for a rest.

Even though he saw Mrs Smith every day when they went in to the farmhouse for their meals, he never got an opportunity to talk to her again. As far as Tommy could see she didn't talk very much to anyone. Every day she seemed to withdraw further and further into herself. She cooked the meals and cleaned the house but other than that she appeared to have no interest in anyone or anything. Tommy wondered if he had upset her by asking about the angel; he wished now he hadn't said anything.

Then early one morning, just as the workers were waking up, the door of the barn burst open and Mr Smith rushed in. He informed them that his wife was missing. She had got up at six o'clock. He assumed she had gone out to feed the hens as she did every morning; but when he went out there was no sign of her. He'd spent the past half hour searching the farmyard and outbuildings without success. All that day the workers and neighbours searched the farm and surrounding area. Then at seven o'clock in the evening their worst fears were realised when her body was found in a river about two miles from the farmhouse.

Everyone was upset by the death of Mrs Smith. She had been well liked by workers and neighbours alike. In her younger days she had been an out-going, and sociable type of person, but they all agreed that she had never recovered from the loss of her only child.

As soon as he heard the news James decided the best thing to do was take Tommy home to Leitrim. This was no place for a seven year old boy now; he'd be better off at home with his mother and sisters. He would come back to attend the funeral and stay as long as Mr Smith needed him on the farm. Even though Tommy had enjoyed is stay at the farm he was glad to hear he was going home. Knowing about little Daniel's death had been bad enough, but now that Mrs Smith had died as well he felt he had enough of the place. Before he fell asleep that night his thoughts turned once again to the angel. Mrs Smith had said she was looking after it for Daniel. But now that she was dead he was worried that there'd be nobody to take care of it.

The following morning his father gathered up Tommy's clothes and put them into his bag. Just as they were about to leave Mr Smith came across the yard to say goodbye to him. Tommy was still thinking about the angel, so he plucked up courage and asked him if he could take it home with him. To his delight, Mr Smith agreed, so Tommy ran into the kitchen, took down the angel and stuffed it into his bag. One of the workmen drove them to the bus stop in Mr Smith's van and they caught the bus for home.

From that day on Tommy kept the angel on the little table beside his bed. Even when he grew up and left home he always kept it with him. When he passed away over seventy years later it was his wish that it be buried with him. Perhaps he hoped, that by taking it with him on his final journey, he could at last return it to its rightful owner - his little brother, Daniel.

FIRST LOVE

In was a warm Sunday evening in July Nineteen fifty three.   Two brothers, Kevin and Jerry, were cycling along the narrow country road. They were on their way to a dancehall which was situated about ten miles from their home.   Kevin who was in his early twenties was well used to attending social gatherings, but for Jerry who was only eighteen it was his first time. In fact, he was lucky to be going at all.

Earlier in the evening when he went to get his bicycle from the shed he realised he had a puncture. Rushing into the kitchen he took the repair kit from the drawer in the dresser only to discover, to his dismay, that there were no patches left. Damn! he thought, what am I going to do now? He'd been looking forward all week to the dance.   The only other bicycle in the place was a new one which his father had purchased recently for himself. Jerry wondered if he'd lend it to him. He made his way into the parlour where Paddy was reading the newspaper.

"Dad, could you do me a favour?" he asked nervously.

"What kind of favour?" asked his father putting down the paper.

"Could you lend me your bike?"

"You know as well as I do, I don't give that bicycle to anyone. Where do you want to go anyway?"

"I'm supposed to be going to the dance tonight with Kevin. Remember I told you about it last week."

"Aye, I remember alright," said his father.

Paddy knew that Jerry had been looking forward all week to going to this dance, so he decided for once to break his own rule and give him the bicycle.

"Oh alright, you can have it for this time but make sure you take good care of it."

Jerry couldn't believe his ears. "Thanks Dad, I'll mind it like a baby" he exclaimed as he hurried off to get ready for the dance.

When they finally arrived at the dancehall they parked their bicycles along with all the others and made their way to the door. There they joined the queue to pay for their tickets. Jerry was a bit surprised to see that it was mostly men who were in the queue. Were there going to be any women there, he wondered. When he got inside he saw that the women were already in the hall. They sat around the sides on long forms chatting to each other and discreetly eyeing up the men as they entered. The men stood at the bottom of the hall, no doubt also eyeing up the women.

Then suddenly the band started to play and it wasn't long until several couples were out on the floor. For a while Jerry just stood and watched what everyone else was doing. He felt a bit shy about asking anyone out to dance. Eventually, however, he saw a good looking girl around his own age sitting with a friend. He wanted to ask her to dance but wasn't sure if he could pluck up the courage. Then somebody asked her friend out and she was sitting all alone. When he thought about it afterwards he couldn't remember approaching her, all he knew was that somehow the two of them ended up dancing together for the rest of the night.

She told him her name was Margaret and the girl she was with was her older sister, Alice. Like him, it was her first time at a dance. She said their parents had warned her big sister to look after her and make sure she didn't get into any trouble. It was obvious to Jerry that Alice was doing her duty as she seemed to be watching them like a hawk all night. The time flew by and before long the band was playing the National Anthem. The instant the music stopped Alice rushed over.

"Come on Margaret," she said, grabbing her by the arm. "We have a lift home, but they won't wait for us, we have to go now this very minute."

Not wanting to make a scene, there was nothing Margaret could do but follow her sister across the floor. Jerry had hoped to ask her if he could see her again but now there was no chance of that. As he stood there and watched the two of them disappear into the night he wondered if he'd ever see Margaret again.

After that night Jerry became a regular at all the dances for miles around. Sometimes a group of lads would cycle fifteen or twenty miles to a dance. He felt sure that sooner or later he'd meet Margaret again but there was no sign of her anywhere he went.

Meanwhile life at home went on as usual. The two brothers worked with their father on their small farm which consisted of about forty acres. The farm was scarcely big enough to support them all, but they had to make do as there was no employment to be found in the area. Some years previously, in order to supplement the income from the land, their father had bought a threshing mill. Starting in October every year he'd travel the countryside for miles threshing corn on farms both big and small. He took Kevin with him when he was old enough. Sometimes they mightn't come back for a fortnight and Jerry and his mother would look after things at home while they were away.

Then one year Paddy decided to take a break from the threshing, so he asked Jerry to go in his place. Jerry was only too delighted to take on the job. It'd be a change from the humdrum life on the farm. They travelled around to several farms and everything was going well. In the evening when they had finished work they'd sometimes take the threshing mill on to the next farm, so that they'd be ready to make an early start in the morning. If there was a spare room in the house they'd sleep there for the night. Otherwise, they'd spend the night in the hay barn.

One evening in November they arrived at a farmhouse at about ten o'clock at night. When they had manoeuvred the mill safely into the haggard, they were invited into the kitchen for the supper. As they were eating the woman of the house, Mrs Maloney, informed them there was a small room upstairs where they could sleep. They thanked her and said they'd have an early night as they had to be up at cockcrow the following morning; there was a heavy day's work ahead. This was in the days before the electric light, so Mrs Maloney carried a candle up the stairs and showed them to their room. Wishing them a good night's sleep, she placed the candle on top of the chest of drawers and disappeared back down to the kitchen. The room was tiny with the double bed taking up most of the space. However, that didn't bother them. Anything was better than sleeping outside in the hay barn. Manoeuvring carefully they managed to get undressed, and it wasn't long until they were both sleeping soundly in the comfortable bed.

The following morning Jerry woke to the sound of the rooster crowing outside in the yard. Dawn was just beginning to break as he got out of bed to check the alarm clock. It was just gone six o'clock. He fished around in the semi-darkness for his clothes.

"Come on Kevin," he called, "Time to get up!"

Jerry never had any problem getting up in the morning. Kevin, on the other hand, always wanted a few minutes extra in bed. It didn't matter what time he woke up, it was always the same; he couldn't get out of bed straight away. Sometimes this annoyed Jerry, especially on a morning like this when there was so much work to be done.

"Just give me five minutes," he pleaded as he pulled the blankets over his head. "Then I'll get up, I promise."

"Ok, five minutes, if you're not up then I'll drag you out of it."

Jerry pulled on his shirt and jumper. Next, he started to put on his trousers and that's when things went wrong. Lifting up his right foot he leaned back against the wall to balance himself and bang! The next thing he knew he was lying on the flat of his back. He heard the voices of women screaming and running feet. With no idea what had happened and unable to move he lay there on the floor in a state of shock. After a couple of minutes he saw Kevin peering down at him.

"Are you ok?" he asked, "here, give me your hand and I'll pull you up."

Kevin pulled him to his feet but he was very confused.

"What happened?"

"The wall you leaned against wasn't really a wall but a curtain dividing the room. There were obviously a couple of women sleeping in the other part. Judging by their screams I'd say they got a terrible fright."

After a few minutes Jerry regained his senses and when he looked around he saw that what Kevin had said was true. The brothers dreaded going down to the kitchen after what had happened but there was nothing for it but face the music. After all, it wasn't their fault.

They made their way down the stairs and through the hallway. When they got to the kitchen door they looked in and saw Mrs Maloney and two young women sitting at the table having their breakfast.

"Good morning boys," said Mrs Maloney smiling "I hope you are alright after that little mishap this morning. My two daughters here got the fright of their lives, but they've recovered now and sure there's no harm done. Sit down there and I'll have your breakfast ready in a minute."

The boys felt awkward. However, they sat down and managed to make some light conversation with the two girls and their mother. As he sat there Jerry had a strange feeling. Something about one of the girls seemed vaguely familiar to him. Then he thought I'm probably imagining it. After what happened this morning I wouldn't be surprised if my mind was playing tricks on me. He didn't have long to think about it as the two girls soon left the kitchen saying they had work to do.

After breakfast the brothers hurried out to the haggard to get ready for the day's threshing. Before long, as was the custom at the time, several neighbours arrived with pitchforks on their shoulders to help out. By nine o'clock the place was a hive of activity. Later in the morning, when the workers were beginning to feel thirsty, they were glad to see the two girls coming from the house carrying refreshments. As Jerry watched them approaching, he suddenly realised why one of them looked familiar. She was the girl he had met at the dance! She came over and handed him a drink.

"Thanks," he said, "I don't know if you remember, but I think we've met before."

"Oh yes, we met before alright," she replied, laughing "at six o'clock this morning, when you came crashing into our room without an invitation."

"No, I don't mean that, I think we met a few years ago. I hope you don't mind me asking, but what's your name?

"Margaret, and that's my younger sister Nora over there."

"I was right, we have met before!"

Jerry reminded her of the night they had spent together at the dance and how her sister had dragged her away at the end of the night.

"Oh yes, I remember now," said Margaret. "I often

wondered if we'd ever meet again."

Later that evening when all the work was done they chatted again and before Jerry left they made a date for the following week-end.

Jerry and Margaret are now thirty years married. Whenever anyone asks them how they met, Margaret always says that Jerry came charging into her room one night while she was sleeping and carried her off on a white steed. He agrees with her version of the story and says that she has never given him cause to regret his daring deed – well, not yet anyway!

THE BOARDING SCHOOL

It could almost be said that Jenny O'Rourke had an idyllic childhood growing up in rural Ireland in the nineteen-sixties. Jenny lived on a small farm and attended the local school. The summer holidays were spent roaming the fields with her younger sister, Elsie, and brothers, Daniel and Robert. Climbing trees, picking blackberries and fishing in the little stream were all part of the long carefree summer days. No matter how early they got up the morning there was never enough time in the day to fit in all the things they wanted to do.

Of course, as with all good things in life, nothing lasts forever and one day when Jenny was twelve years old a dark cloud appeared on the horizon. Her mother, who had always been so full of life and energy, became unwell and had to stay in bed. At first they all thought it was just a cold and she'd be up and about again in no time. Sadly, it wasn't to be and her condition deteriorated. Eventually she was taken into hospital where she passed away a couple of weeks later. The whole family was devastated. Their father, Michael, couldn't manage on his own so Jenny's older sister, Lizzie, stayed at home from school to help look after the family. Their Aunt Hannah who lived nearby kept an eye on them too and often called in to make sure they were doing ok.

One evening in June Jenny was in the yard kicking a ball around with the younger children when Aunt Hannah came cycling up the road on her High Nelly, parked it against the gable end of the house, and hurried into the kitchen. About ten minutes later her father came to the door and called her in. Jenny wondered if she was in trouble but couldn't think of anything she had done wrong. In fact, they had all been on their best behaviour since their mother died. They just didn't have the heart to get up to their usual antics.

"Sit down Jenny, there's something we want to talk to you about," said Michael.
Jenny sat down and looked from one to the other wondering what was coming next.
"How would you like to go to a boarding school in September? asked Aunt Hannah.
Jenny was puzzled. "A boarding school?"
"Well, now that you've finished primary school, you'll

have to start secondary school in September."

"I know that," said Jenny "but can't I go to the secondary school in the town, like Lizzie?"

"Lizzie won't be going back in September, so we think it's too far for you to cycle on your own. I've had a word with Father Thompson and he says he can get you into a good boarding school up the country. You'll get a much better education and you won't have to be cycling the roads in all weathers. What do you think?"

Jenny turned to her father. "Dad, how can you afford to send me to a boarding school? Don't those places cost a lot of money?"

"Don't worry about that Jenny." replied her father. "Father Thompson knows the nuns well and they've agreed to put aside the fees. Apparently, the school is doing very well, so they can afford to take in a certain number of non fee-paying students every year. This year you're to be one of the lucky ones."

Jenny was dumbfounded. It was just a few weeks since her mother had passed away and she was struggling to adjust to life without her. Now, everything was about to change again. She wished her Aunt Hannah and Father Thompson would mind their own business and let them get on with their lives. However, she didn't want to kick up a fuss either, as she knew her father had enough problems already and he was only trying to do his best. So she agreed to go along with the plan.

Jenny was determined to enjoy the summer

months with her family. Every day she looked after the three younger children while Lizzie got on with the housework. They roamed the fields and enjoyed all their usual activities. One day in August, as they sat beneath the old apple tree in the yard, she decided to tell her sister, Elsie, who was two years younger than her, that she would be going to a boarding school in September. At first Elsie didn't know what a boarding school was, but when Jenny explained it to her she became upset and started crying.

"It's not fair! First Mammy went away and now you're leaving us as well." she wailed, the tears streaming down her face.

Jenny put her arm around Elsie as she tried to comfort her. "But Christmas won't be long coming around and we'll all see each other again. And there's something important I want you to do for me. Promise me you'll take good care of the boys while I'm away."

"But won't Lizzie be taking care of them?"

"Of course she will. But Lizzie will be busy in the house so you can keep an eye on them when they're outside, just so they don't get up to too much mischief. Do you think you can do that?"

Elsie nodded her head, as the ghost of a smile slowly spread across her face.

"Good, that's settled then. Now let's go and see if there are any eggs to be collected."

The two girls jumped to their feet and holding hands they skipped their way across the yard towards the henhouse.

The rest of August flew by and soon it was time for Jenny to leave for the boarding school. She quickly said goodbye to the other children promising them she'd see them at Christmas. Her Aunt Hannah got into the front passenger seat beside her father while Jenny and her suitcase occupied the back seat. Then Michael started up the old Volkswagen and, with a quick wave to the little group standing in the yard, Jenny was on her way to her new abode.

After travelling for almost three hours they finally arrived at their destination. Michael took Jenny's suitcase and the three of them walked up to the big brown door at the front of the building. Michael knocked and the door was opened immediately by a young nun. Glancing at Jenny and the suitcase she beckoned to them to come inside. Showing them into a small parlour, she told them to sit down while she went to find the Reverend Mother. A few minutes later the parlour door swung open and a tall, haughty-looking nun, who appeared to be in her late fifties, swept into the room.

"Good Afternoon," she said, looking her three visitors up and down "I'm Mother Aloysius, Mother Superior of the convent. And who have I the pleasure of meeting, may I ask?"

Aunt Hannah acted as spokesperson for them all. "I'm Hannah Kelly, this is my brother Michael O'Rourke and his daughter Jenny who is here to start her first year as a boarder in the school."

"Oh, I see. You're very welcome," replied the Reverend Mother, with a sweet smile and a brief nod towards Jenny. Now, would you all like a cup of tea after your journey?"

"We'd love a cup," said Aunt Hannah, "we've been travelling for almost three hours and to tell you the truth we're parched with the thirst."

"I'll get sister Margaretta to bring some without delay. Oh by the way," she coughed delicately, "before I do that, there's just the little matter of the fee to be taken care of. It's always been our policy to collect half the money at the beginning of the year and the rest when the school re-opens in January. So if you can give me a cheque now Mr O'Rourke, I'll be only too happy to write you a receipt."

As she said this she fished in the pocket of her habit and pulled out a receipt book and pen. Michael and Hannah looked at each other in dismay; there must be some mistake.

"I'm sorry Reverend Mother, said Hannah, "but there seems to be a misunderstanding. You see, our parish priest, Fr Thompson, made an arrangement for Jenny to come here as a non-fee paying student. Apparently, you take in a certain number every year who can't afford to pay."

As soon as Mother Aloysius heard this her whole manner changed. "Oh," she said impatiently, "so she's one of those! Why didn't you say so earlier and not be wasting my time? Personally, I'm not in favour of taking in students free of charge at all. It was the bishop's idea. He insisted that with the school doing so well we should take in a certain number of 'special cases' every year." She turned and looked critically at Jenny. "Now that you're here I hope you'll show appreciation for our generosity and be on your best behaviour at all times. And now" she said, moving towards the door, "I'll have to ask you two to leave. I'm very busy and have quite a number of people to meet today."

"But what about the tea?" asked Aunt Hannah hopefully.

" I'm sorry," replied Mother Aloysius abruptly, "I forgot that the kitchen staff have the afternoon off, so I'm afraid there won't be any tea after all."

From this first meeting with Mother Aloysius, Jenny had a feeling that they weren't going to like each other very much. However, she didn't have time to think about it that evening. As soon as her father and aunt had left she was handed over to the care of another student, called Marie, whose job it was to show her around. When she finally got to bed that night she was exhausted and slept like a log. The following morning she woke to the sound of a bell ringing. She jumped out of bed along with all the other girls in the dormitory. After washing their hands and faces in cold water, they got dressed and quickly made their way to the chapel for seven o'clock Mass. When Mass was over, it was back to the dormitory to make their beds and tidy up, and then down to the refectory for breakfast. After breakfast they had to go straight to the classroom to begin the day's lessons. The whole day was organised like this, with almost military precision, leaving only two hours free in the evening for recreation.

From the very first day Jenny knew that she wasn't going to like this place at all. While she did make friends with a couple of other first years, most of the students were from well-to-do families and seemed so much more sophisticated than her. The building was cold. The food was terrible and there wasn't nearly enough of it. In fact, she went to bed hungry almost every night. The students were allowed to write home. However, the letters were required to be left open so that the nuns could read them before posting. This eliminated the chance of any negative comments reaching the parents, at least during the school term.

All of these factors resulted in Jenny taking an extreme dislike to the school. However, her biggest problem of all was Mother Aloysius herself. Very few of the students liked her, but she seemed to take an unwarranted dislike to Jenny and never missed an opportunity to make her feel inferior in front of the others.

One day at dinnertime the girls were all in the refectory when Mother Aloysius swept in on one of her random inspections. She walked slowly up and down the room scanning the tables as she went to make sure everything was in order. As she approached the table where Jenny was sitting with five other girls, she suddenly stopped and roared in a loud voice "Jenny O'Rourke, stand up". Jenny stood up, wondering what she had done wrong.

"Why did I ask you to stand up?"

"I ..I.. don't know, Mother" answered Jenny nervously.

"Of course you don't, but then, you never know anything do you?"

Mother Aloysius noticed one of her favourite students sitting at the same table.

"Jacinta," she said, "can you tell us why I asked Jenny to stand up?"

"She was holding her knife and fork in the wrong hands, Mother." answered Jacinta smugly.

"Precisely. Thank you Jacinta."

She turned on Jenny again. "How is it that you are the only girl in the room who doesn't know how to use a knife and fork properly? Perhaps this will help you remember the next time."

As she said this, she picked up the milk jug from the table and poured the contents over Jenny's head. There were some nervous giggles from other students as Jenny stood there with the milk running down her head and face and dripping on to her uniform. The tears stung her eyes, but she held them back determined not to let Mother Aloysius have the satisfaction of seeing her cry.

After that incident Jenny tried harder than ever to avoid Mother Aloysius. The only thing that kept her going was the thought that she would soon be going home for Christmas. She hoped that when she told her father how much she hated the place he wouldn't send her back after the holidays.

A few days before Christmas Jenny stood in the hallway, along with several other girls, waiting for her father to come and collect her. After what seemed like an eternity she heard her name being called and when she hurried to the door and saw her father standing there she couldn't have been any happier. The nightmare was over, at least for now, and she felt she could breathe again. When they arrived home that evening Jenny got a hearty welcome from the rest of the family; they were all so happy to see her. Without delay she got straight into helping with the preparations for Christmas.

Halfway through the holidays Jenny decided to a have word with her father about going back to school.

"Dad," she asked nervously, "do I absolutely have to go back to that boarding school in January?

"I've been meaning to talk to you about that." replied her father, "There's a bus service to the local school beginning in the New Year. The bus will pick you up at the gate and bring you back again in the evening and it only costs ten shillings a week. Unless of course, you really want to go back," he added, with a smile, "now that would be a different matter entirely."

This was the best news Jenny could have hoped for; she'd never have to go back to that awful place again. I must be the luckiest girl in Ireland, she thought. And so Jenny's brief experience of boarding school life came to an end. For a long time afterwards she had nightmares about Mother Aloysius and she often wished there was some way she could get even with her. As time went by, however, and she was busy getting on with her life, she thought about her less and less.

Then, out of the blue, thirty years later Jenny came face to face with her old adversary again. She and her sister Elsie, who were now both married with families of their own, went on a short break to the West of Ireland. On the way home Jenny who was driving decided to take a slight detour which would bring them through the town where the boarding school was situated. On arriving she drove down the street and parked the car opposite the building. She was surprised to see how little it had changed over the years. The high gate and railings were still the same as well as the big brown door which had swallowed her up all those years ago.

It was late afternoon and the street was quiet. In fact, there was nobody around expect for an old nun who was painting the white railings in front of the building. She had a can of paint on the ground beside her and appeared to be engrossed in what she was doing.

"That's her!" exclaimed Jenny excitedly.

"Who?" Elsie asked.

"Mother Aloysius!"

Jenny opened the car door.

"Where are you going?" asked Elsie, alarmed.

"I'm going to talk to her," replied Jenny as she got out of the car, slammed the door and marched across the street. Elsie quickly jumped out of the passenger seat and followed close behind.

"Good afternoon Mother Aloysius, I'm one of your past students, do you remember me?" asked Jenny.

Mother Aloysius turned slowly, paintbrush in hand, and looked her up and down. "Indeed I don't." She replied dismissively "You hardly expect me to remember everyone who passed through these gates during my time in charge."

Jenny had thought that the passing of the years might have changed Mother Aloysius for the better, but she could see that this was the same cold-hearted woman of thirty years before. There's only one way to get even with her, she thought, and that is to give her a dose of her own medicine. Picking up the can of white paint she was about to empty it over the nun's black habit when Elsie grabbed her by the arm.

"Please Jenny," she begged, "don't do it. She's not worth it. Come on, let's go home".

Jenny realised that her sister was right. After all these years she had finally got her chance to get revenge for the way Mother Aloysius had treated her, but she decided not to take it. Why should she stoop to her level? She would be the bigger person and walk away. So she dropped the paint can, walked back to the car with Elsie, and without another look in Mother Aloysius's direction, drove away.

After that Jenny put the boarding school and Mother Aloysius out of her mind for good. When her own children came to secondary school age she made sure they all went to the local school; she had no wish to put them through a similar ordeal to what she had suffered all those years before.

THE HITCHHIKER

When Charles McSweeney retired as postman in the village of Glenbawn in nineteen sixty-five, he decided to trade-in his old Morris Minor for a brand new Ford Anglia. His wife, Rose, was over the moon and it wasn't long until she convinced him that they should take a holiday in the West of Ireland. They booked into a nice little hotel on the coast and spent a whole week taking in the sea air and enjoying the breath-taking scenery the area had to offer. When the week was up they rather reluctantly packed their bags and started for home. Leaving the hotel about three o'clock in the afternoon, even though it was late October and the days were getting short, they thought they'd have plenty of time to get home before night.

The journey, however, didn't quite go as smoothly

as they had hoped. The road they took on the way home was one they'd never travelled before and it wasn't long until they realised they were lost. Instead of coming to the main road which would bring them towards home they took a wrong turn along the way and found themselves in a remote mountainous region in the middle of nowhere. The only thing they could do was keep going and hope they would eventually get back to the main road. As they travelled on, however, the road narrowed and the terrain became more rugged. As if things weren't bad enough, they noticed that the petrol tank indicator was getting low. If they didn't get to a petrol station soon they'd be going nowhere fast.

Then, the weather which had been sunny and dry when they left their hotel, suddenly changed. It started with a few big drops spattering the windscreen. Then the wind rose, and before long, the rain was lashing the car. Charles was finding it difficult to see the road in front of them.

"Things are going from bad to worse," he grumbled, "all we need now is for the petrol to run out and we'll end up sitting in the car all night." "With a bit of luck," replied Rose, trying to sound more optimistic than she felt, "we'll soon see a sign for a hotel of some sort where we can stay the night." "I hope you're right," Charles retorted, and they continued on for some time in silence.

As they were travelling along a particularly dark stretch of road which was lined with trees on both sides, they suddenly saw a tall slender figure in black standing in the ditch. When the car came close the figure waved frantically as if they wanted them to stop, but Charles kept on driving as if he hadn't noticed.

"That looks like a young girl," said Rose, "I think we should stop and give her a lift. It's not right to leave her there on a night like this."

Anything for a quiet life, thought Charles, as he stopped the car and reversed back a couple of hundred yards. The girl opened the door and got into the back seat.

"Thanks for stopping," she said, "I didn't think I was ever going to get a lift."

"Are you going far?" asked Rose.

"Only a couple of miles, I'll tell you when to let me out."

"Now that you're here maybe you can help us. Do you know if there are any hotels around these parts? We're looking for somewhere to stay the night."

"Actually, you're in luck. My parents run a small hotel; I'm sure they'll be able to put you up."

"That's great. What a coincidence that we should meet you like this."

About ten minutes later the girl instructed them to turn right into an avenue which led up to the hotel. When they reached the building Charles stopped the car and turned off the engine. Rose turned around in her seat to speak to the girl but to her surprise she was gone. She must have jumped out of the car the moment it stopped and ran around the side of the building.

"Well, that was quick," said Rose, "she must have been in a terrible hurry altogether."

"Maybe she wasn't supposed to be out," replied Charles, "and was trying to get back in without her parents knowing. Sure, you'd never know what them young ones would be up to nowadays".

When they knocked at the front door it was opened by a middle-aged gentleman who invited them in. He told them he was George Moorefield, proprietor of the hotel. Luckily, he could provide them with a room for the night. As they were signing their names in the guest book a woman came into the hallway whom he introduced as his wife, Dorothea. When their business with George was finished Dorothea showed them to their room.

The following morning they awoke refreshed from a good night's sleep and made their way down to the dining-room. Half-way through the breakfast Dorothea came in to ask them if they had everything they needed. They assured her that everything was fine. Rose being a curious, or some might even say nosy, sort of person decided this was her opportunity to find out a bit about the hotel.

"Have you been running this hotel for long?" she asked.

"We've been running it for the past twenty years, ever since George's father died and left it to him. However, it's been in my husband's family for almost a hundred and fifty years. It was built in the eighteen twenties and has been passed down through the generations.

"Isn't that wonderful," said Rose, "and I suppose your daughter's generation will be the next to take it over."

Dorothea gave her a strange look, and Rose, thinking she had offended her, hastily added "after your day of course, which won't be for a long time yet."

"I don't know why you should say that," said Dorothea, "we don't have a daughter."

Rose was confused. Why should Mrs Moorefield say she hadn't a daughter when they had been talking to her the previous night? She was just about to pursue the matter further when Charles intervened.

"You'll have to excuse my wife, Mrs Moorefield, when she starts asking questions she doesn't know when to stop. If you don't mind, we have a long way to travel so we'll finish our breakfast and get going."

That put an end to the conversation, and Dorothea hurried off to attend to other guests. Before they left the hotel George gave them instructions on how to get back to the main road and where to find the nearest petrol station. They thanked him for his help and started on their journey.

"There's something strange about that place," said Rose, as they drove down the avenue and out onto the road. "And if you hadn't interrupted so rudely I might have found out what it was,"

"I thought it better not to get involved," replied

Charles, "as the saying goes 'what we don't know can't trouble us'."

About a mile down the road they came to a small church with a priest's house and an adjoining graveyard. If there was one thing Rose couldn't resist it was a visit to a graveyard, so she made Charles stop the car so they could go in and have a quick look around. As they walked down to the bottom of the graveyard Rose spotted the name "Moorefield" engraved on top of a rather ancient looking headstone.

"I wonder if they're the ancestors of the people we stayed with last night," she mused.

With some difficulty she read down through the names and dates on the headstone until she came to the last inscription which read *"also in memory of Rebecca Moorefield who departed this life on 29th October, 1865, aged 19 years R.I.P."* . It wasn't just the name and the youthful age of the girl that struck her. There was something else, and that was the date of her death, which was exactly one hundred years ago the previous day. A strange feeling came over Rose; she knew she just had to find out more about Rebecca Moorefield. Clutching Charles firmly by the arm and giving him no chance to protest, she led him out of the graveyard and straight to the door of the priest's house. She knocked loudly and after a few minutes the door was opened by an elderly priest.

"Good morning," He greeted them, "how can I help you?"

"Good morning Father," replied Rose. "We're looking for information about somebody who is buried in the graveyard, and we wondered if you'd be able to help us."

"Well, I'll certainly do my best. Let's take a walk over there and you can point out the headstone to me."

The three of them walked over to the old headstone. "Moorefield. That grave belongs to a very old family in this parish. In fact, their descendants are still living here. They are the owners of a small hotel situated about a mile from here. What do you want to know about them?"

"Well, it's the young girl, Rebecca, we're interested in really. We were just wondering what happened to her?"

"Ah yes, that was a tragic story." said the priest, as he stooped down to look at the inscription. "According to what I've been told, Rebecca was murdered."

"Murdered?" Rose was stunned.

"It seems she started a relationship with a young man whom her parents didn't approve of. He had a bad name and had been in trouble with the law on several occasions. They forbade her to have anything to do with him, but she used to sneak out at night to meet him. He tried to convince her to steal a large sum of money from her parents so that the two of them could run away together. She agreed to go along with the plan, but at the last minute she confided in her sister who persuaded her not do it. When she told him that she had changed her mind he went crazy and strangled her. Her body was found the next day by the side of the road. The boyfriend disappeared and was never seen in the area again. But that's not the end of the story. They say that Rebecca's ghost has been seen several times over the years near the spot where she was murdered."

Suddenly it all became clear to Rose. She knew now that the young girl they had picked up the previous night wasn't a daughter of George and Dorothea at all, but Rebecca. Rose said a prayer that, having made her way home on the one-hundredth anniversary of her death, Rebecca could finally rest in peace. And her prayers must have been answered, because, from that day on, the ghost of Rebecca Moorefield was never seen again.

BORRIS ON 15TH AUGUST

Johnny Connors sat outside the door of his little caravan on a halting site somewhere in the south-east of Ireland. As he puffed on his old pipe, he thought about the disturbing news he had heard that morning. A neighbour had told him there were rumours going around that the annual fair in Borris, which was held on the 15th of August every year, was to be discontinued.

Johnny was eighty years old. He had attended the fair every year of his life, first with his father and grandfather, and later with his own children and grandchildren. Johnny had seen many changes during his lifetime, and most of the old ways were gone forever. The trip to Borris each year on the 15th of August was one of the few pleasures he had left in life. He met up with family and friends from all over the country and caught up on all the news such as who had died and who had got married during the year. He enjoyed listening to the banter of the horse-traders as they bought and sold; it was just like the old days. And he loved to walk the length of the street and look at all the different goods on offer. He nearly always ended up buying himself a new pair of boots or a top coat. There was nowhere like Borris on the 15th to kit yourself out for the winter. You could always be sure of a bargain. Johnny knew that if he had to live his life in a day – he would spend it in Borris on the 15th August.

As he sat there thinking about the possibility of having no more fairs to go to, he suddenly remembered something he had heard long ago. His father had told him that Queen Elizabeth 1st of England had granted a royal charter for the holding of the fair four hundred years previously. Maybe, thought Johnny, if somebody was to get in touch with her descendent, Queen Elizabeth 2nd, and ask for an extension of the charter, the fair could go ahead indefinitely. The more he thought about it, the more it seemed like a good idea. What would he have to lose anyway? It was worth a try.

Now Johnny wasn't a great hand at the writing himself, so he asked his grandson, Miley, would he write a letter for him. Miley arrived down at Johnny's caravan the following evening with pen and paper.

"Alright Granddad" said Miley "who do you want

to write to?"

"The Queen of England," replied Johnny

"Ah, come on Granddad, I'm in a hurry, I have no time for jokes."

"I'm not joking," said Johnny, looking serious, "I'm writing to the queen of England. Are you ready?"

Miley thought his granddad was losing his marbles, but decided the easiest option was to go along with him. Johnny told him to put his address at the top of the letter. Then he continued:

Your Majesty,

I hope this finds you in good health, I'm grand myself, except for the auld arthritis, but I suppose at eighty, what can you expect.

I wish to inform you of an important matter I believe deserves your attention. There is grave danger that the fair in Borris on 15th August is going to be discontinued. Your predecessor Queen Elizabeth 1st granted a royal charter for the running of this fair 400 years ago. Do you think you could add an extension to the charter that would ensure the fair will continue indefinitely into the future?

I would be most grateful, Madam, for your attention to this matter. It would mean an awful lot, not only to me, but to all the travelling people of Ireland and the generations to come.

Yours sincerely

Johnny Connors (Mr)

"Now," said Johnny, "you can look up the Queen's address on that internet yoke you're always talking about, and post it off to her straight away."

Miley did as he was told and posted the letter the next day. About a month passed and Johnny had given up hope of getting a reply. Then one day a letter arrived with the Buckingham Palace stamp on it. He asked Miley to come down to the caravan and read it for him. Miley opened the letter and read:

Dear Mr Connors,

Thank you for your letter. I am not normally in the habit of replying to correspondence personally, but as this appears to be such a grave matter, I have made an exception. Unfortunately, it is not in my remit to grant an indefinite extension to the charter for the fair in Borris. I do, however, appreciate the importance of this annual event, especially to the travelling people of your country. Therefore, I have decided to add another 400 years to the existing charter. I doubt it will make any difference to either you or I what happens after that. And you never know, Mr Connors, I may take a trip over there myself someday to see what all the fuss is about; they tell me it's a great day out entirely.

Yours sincerely,

Queen Elizabeth 2 nd of England

That was five years ago and Johnny is still going to the fair every year. As he walks up and down the street looking for bargains, he always keeps an eye out for Queen Elizabeth. He hasn't spotted her so far, but who knows, maybe one day. After all, stranger things have happened.

ABOUT THE AUTHOR

Mary Nolan lives near Borris in County Carlow. She loves reading and writing about life in rural Ireland in times gone by. Mary recently completed a Creative Writing Course at The People's College, Dublin and has had her work published in books and magazines. This is her third book of short stories.

Printed in Poland
by Amazon Fulfillment
Poland Sp. z o.o., Wrocław